Weenie

featuring Frank & Beans

MAD ABOUT MEATLOAF

WRITTEN BY
Maureen Fergus

ILLUSTRATED BY
Alexandra Bye

tundra

FOR MY DARLING HANNAH,
BECAUSE YOU ARE WONDERFUL — MF

FOR OLIVER, MY FAVORITE GOLDEN RETRIEVER,
ADVENTURE BUDDY, STUDIO MATE AND BEST FRIEND — AB

Text copyright © 2021 by Maureen Fergus
Illustrations copyright © 2021 by Alexandra Bye

Tundra Books, an imprint of Penguin Random House Canada Young Readers,
a division of Penguin Random House of Canada Limited

Library and Archives Canada Cataloguing in Publication

Title: Mad about meatloaf / Maureen Fergus ; Alexandra Bye, illustrator.
Names: Fergus, Maureen, author. | Bye, Alexandra, illustrator.
Description: Series statement: Weenie featuring Frank and Beans
Identifiers: Canadiana (print) 20200372904 | Canadiana (ebook) 20200372963
ISBN 9780735267916 (hardcover) | ISBN 9780735267923 (EPUB)
Subjects: LCGFT: Graphic novels.
Classification: LCC PN6733.F47 M33 2021 | DDC j741.5/971—dc23

Published simultaneously in the United States of America by Tundra Books of
Northern New York, an imprint of Penguin Random House Canada Young Readers,
a division of Penguin Random House of Canada Limited

Library of Congress Control Number: 2020948999

Edited by Samantha Swenson
Designed by John Martz
The artwork in this book was rendered with Photoshop and dog hair.
The text was set in DigitalStrip BB.
Image of California Nebula on page 18 courtesy NASA/JPL-Caltech

Printed in China

www.penguinrandomhouse.ca

1   2   3   4   5   25   24   23   22   21

Penguin
Random House
tundra | TUNDRA BOOKS

MAD ABOUT MEATLOAF

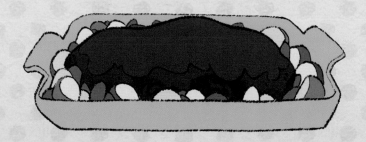

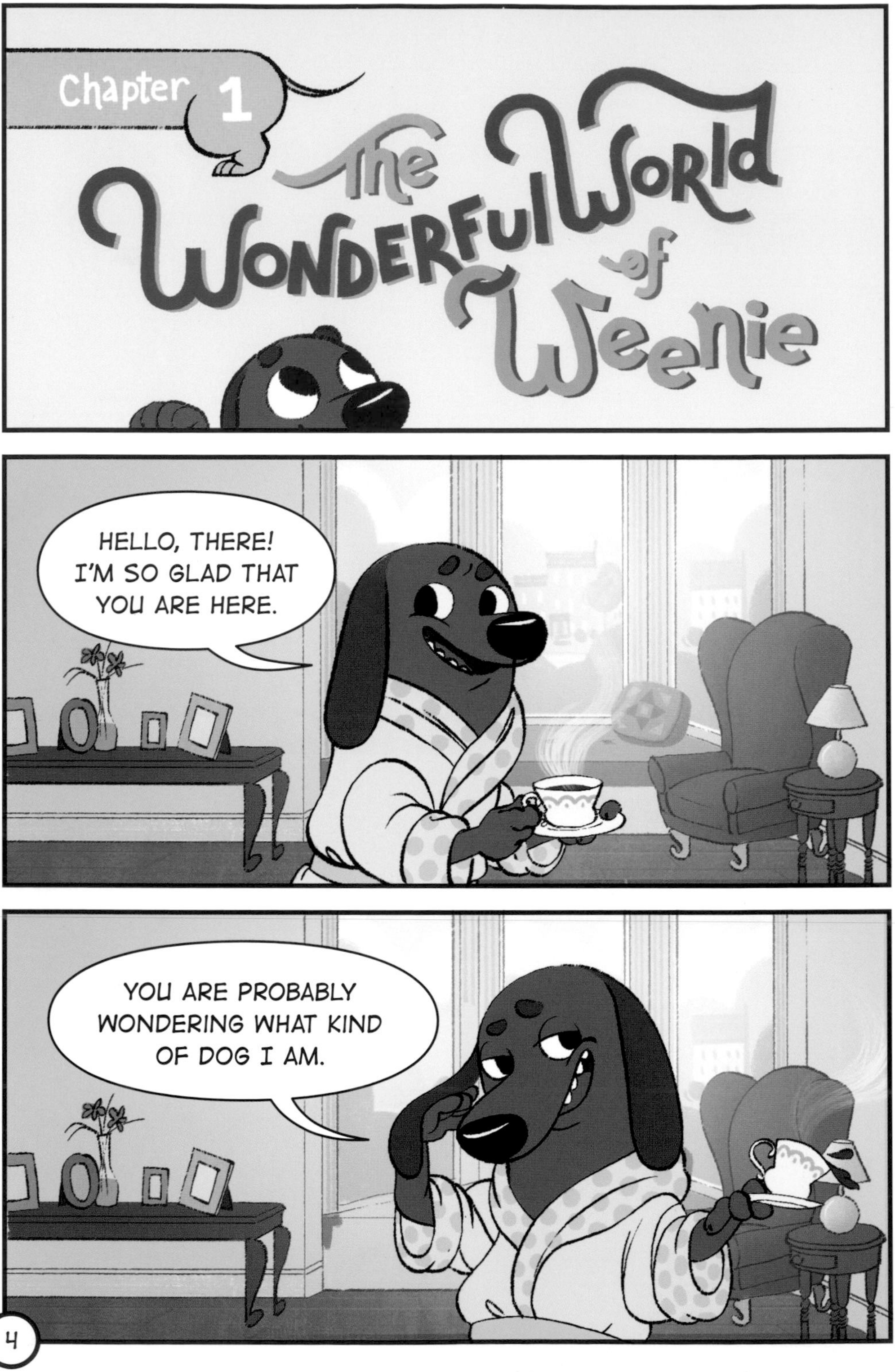
Chapter 1
The Wonderful World of Weenie
HELLO, THERE! I'M SO GLAD THAT YOU ARE HERE.
YOU ARE PROBABLY WONDERING WHAT KIND OF DOG I AM.

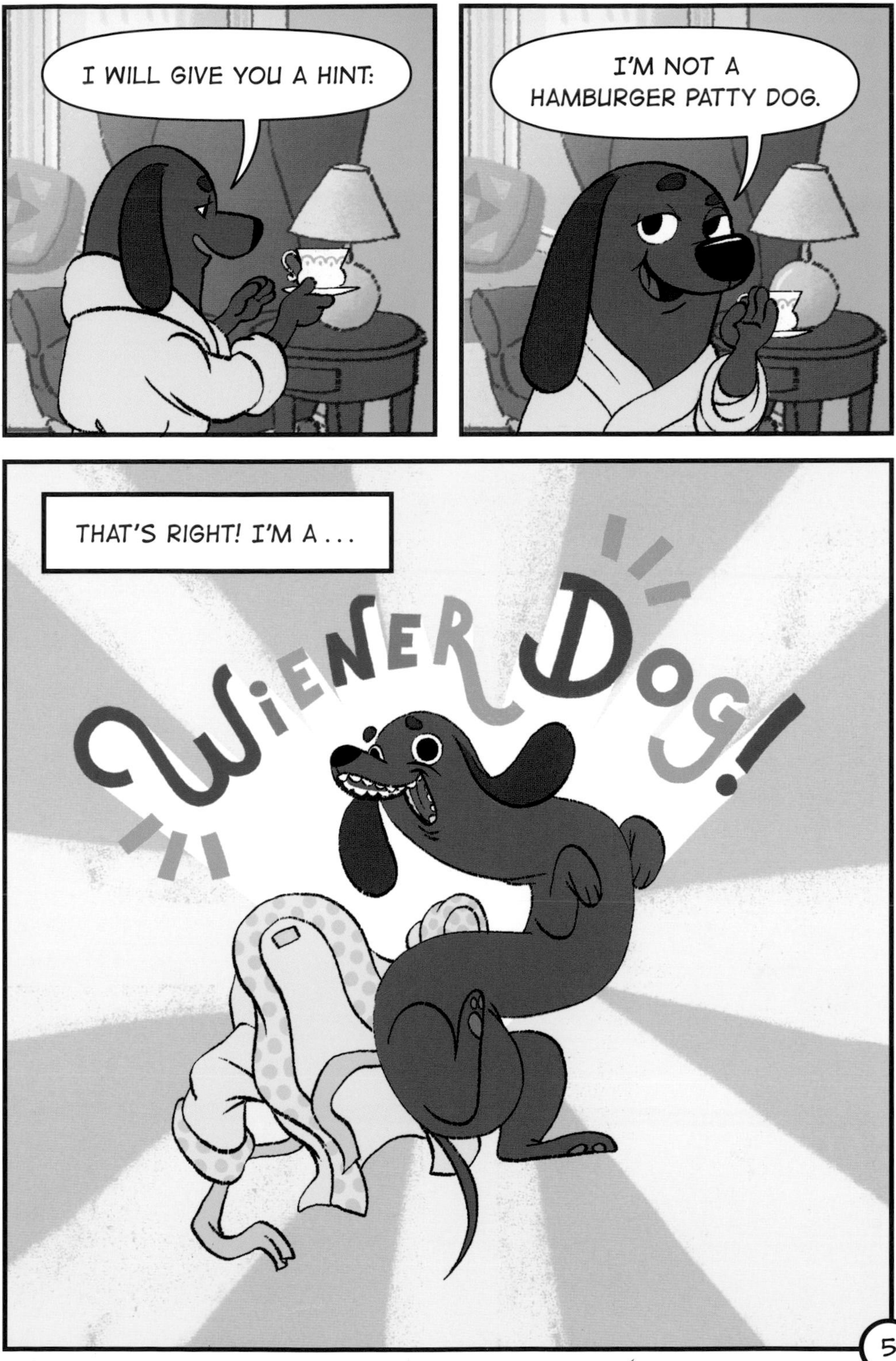
I WILL GIVE YOU A HINT:
I'M NOT A HAMBURGER PATTY DOG.
THAT'S RIGHT! I'M A . . .
WIENER DOG!

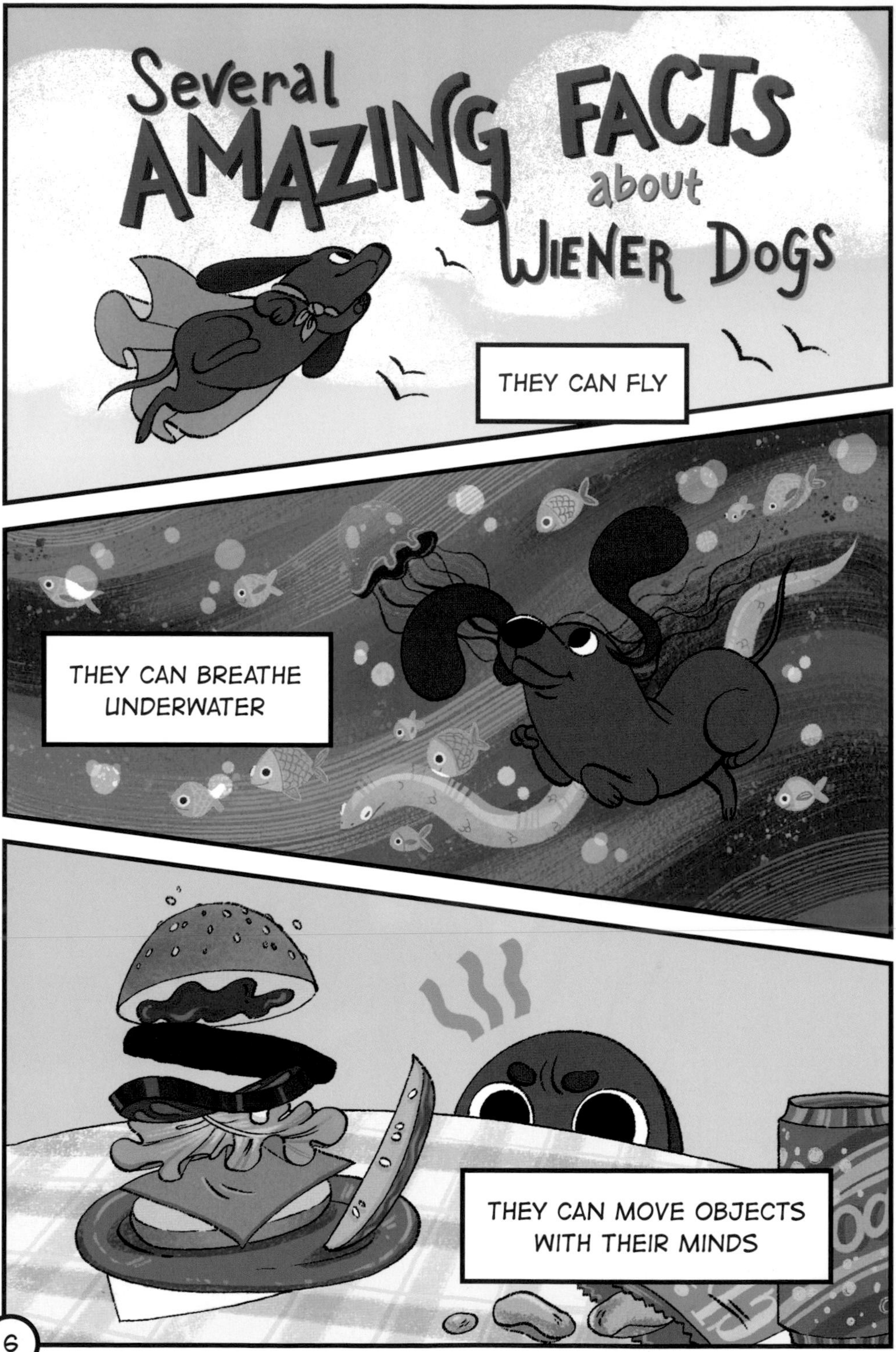
Several AMAZING FACTS about WIENER DOGS
THEY CAN FLY
THEY CAN BREATHE UNDERWATER
THEY CAN MOVE OBJECTS WITH THEIR MINDS

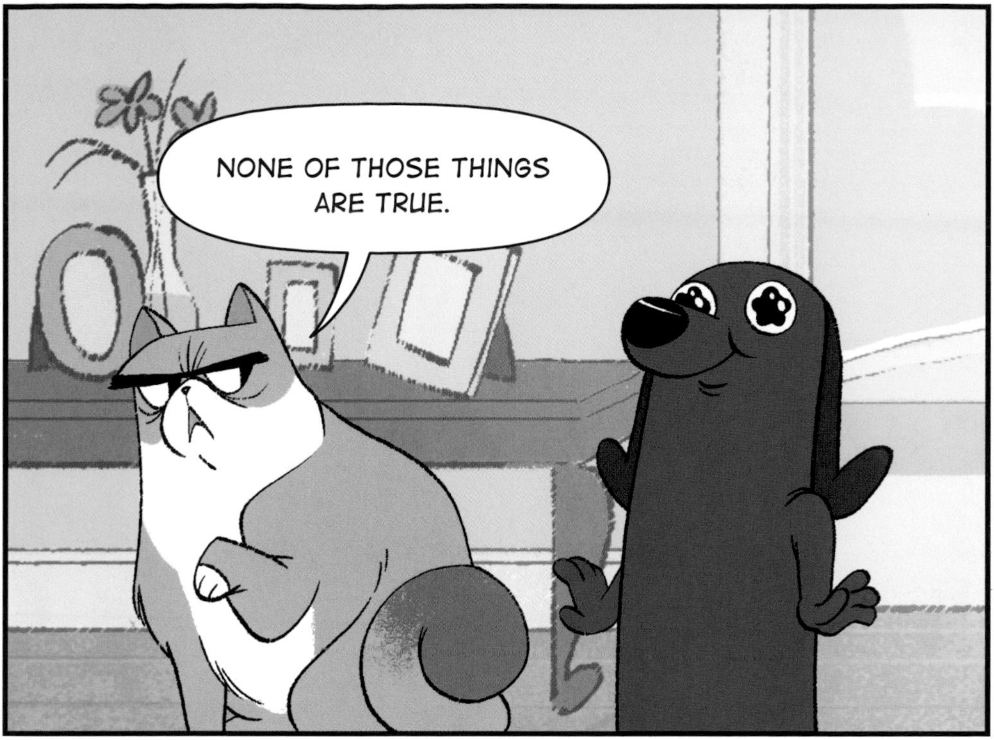
NONE OF THOSE THINGS ARE TRUE.

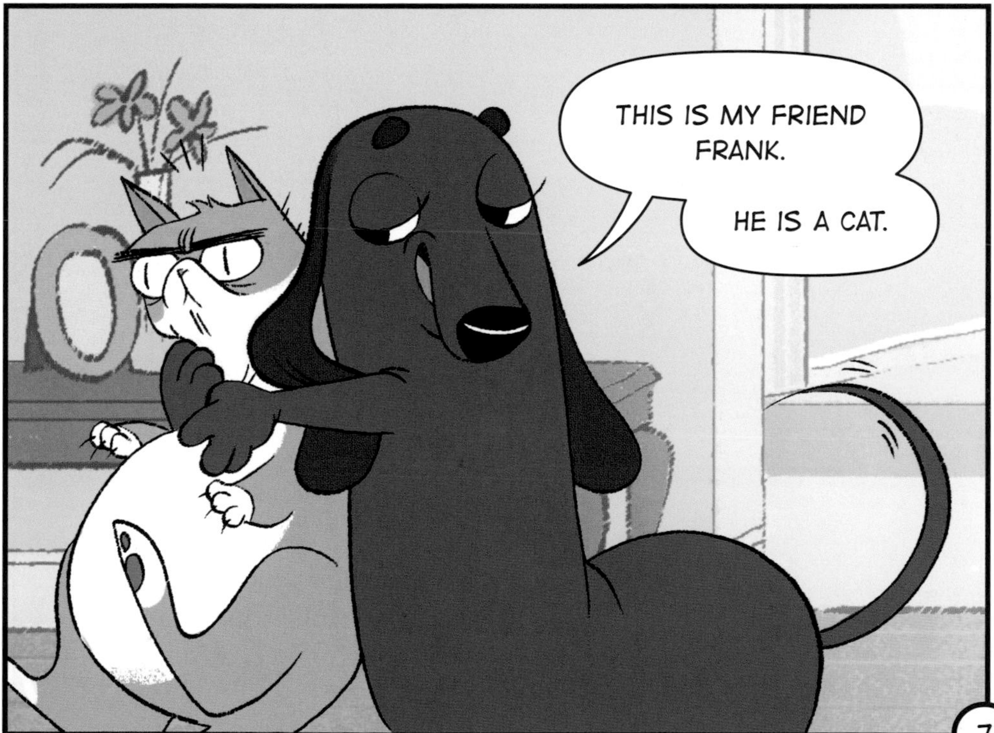
THIS IS MY FRIEND FRANK.
HE IS A CAT.

Some things you Should know about CATS

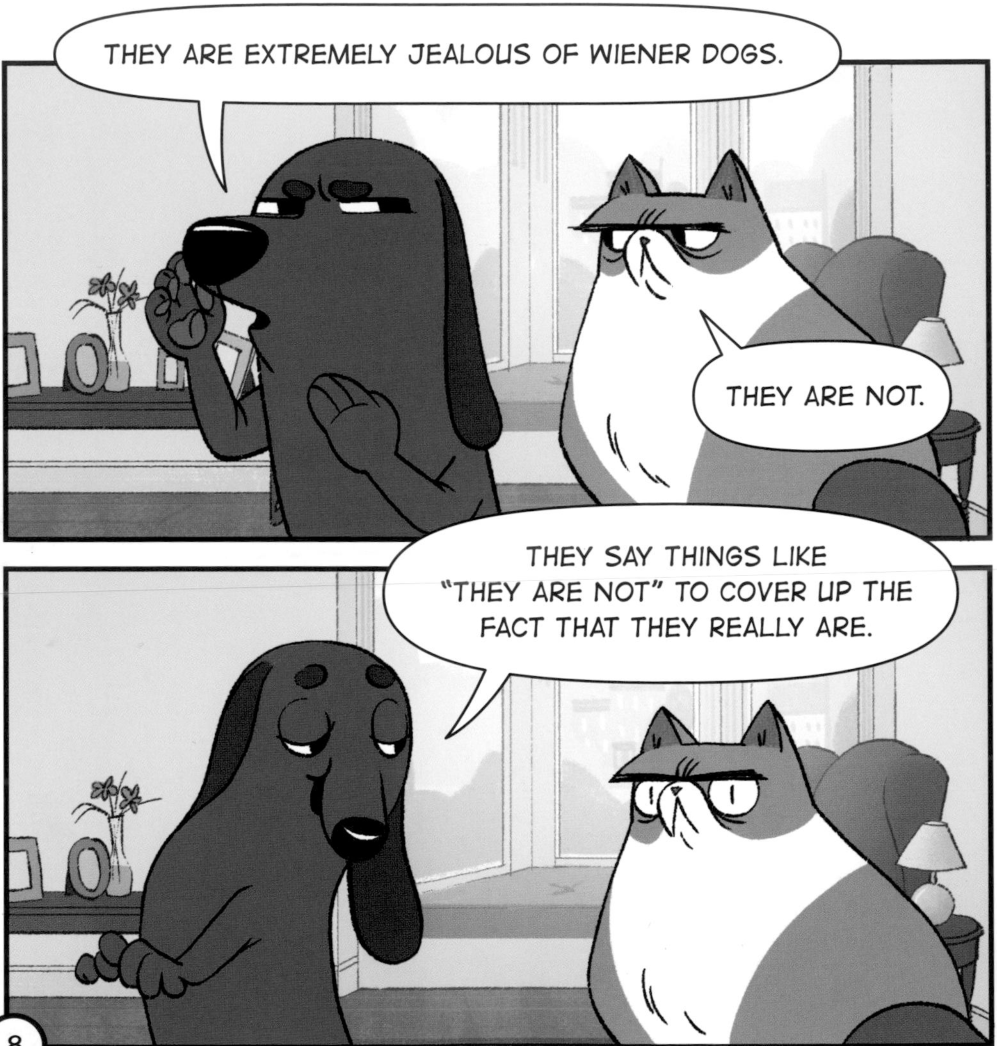
THEY ARE EXTREMELY JEALOUS OF WIENER DOGS.
THEY ARE NOT.
THEY SAY THINGS LIKE "THEY ARE NOT" TO COVER UP THE FACT THAT THEY REALLY ARE.

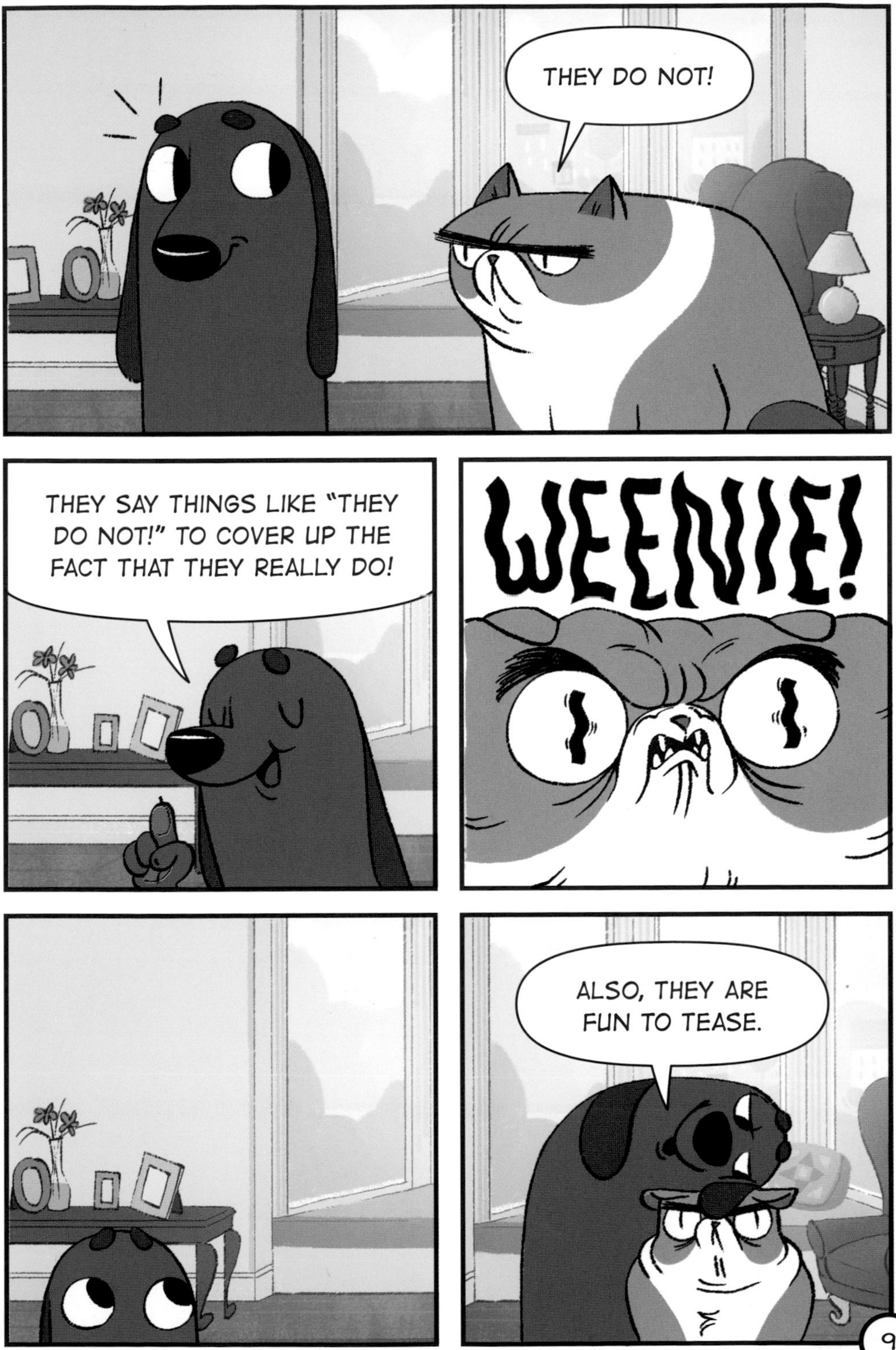
THEY DO NOT!
THEY SAY THINGS LIKE "THEY DO NOT!" TO COVER UP THE FACT THAT THEY REALLY DO!
WEENIE!
ALSO, THEY ARE FUN TO TEASE.

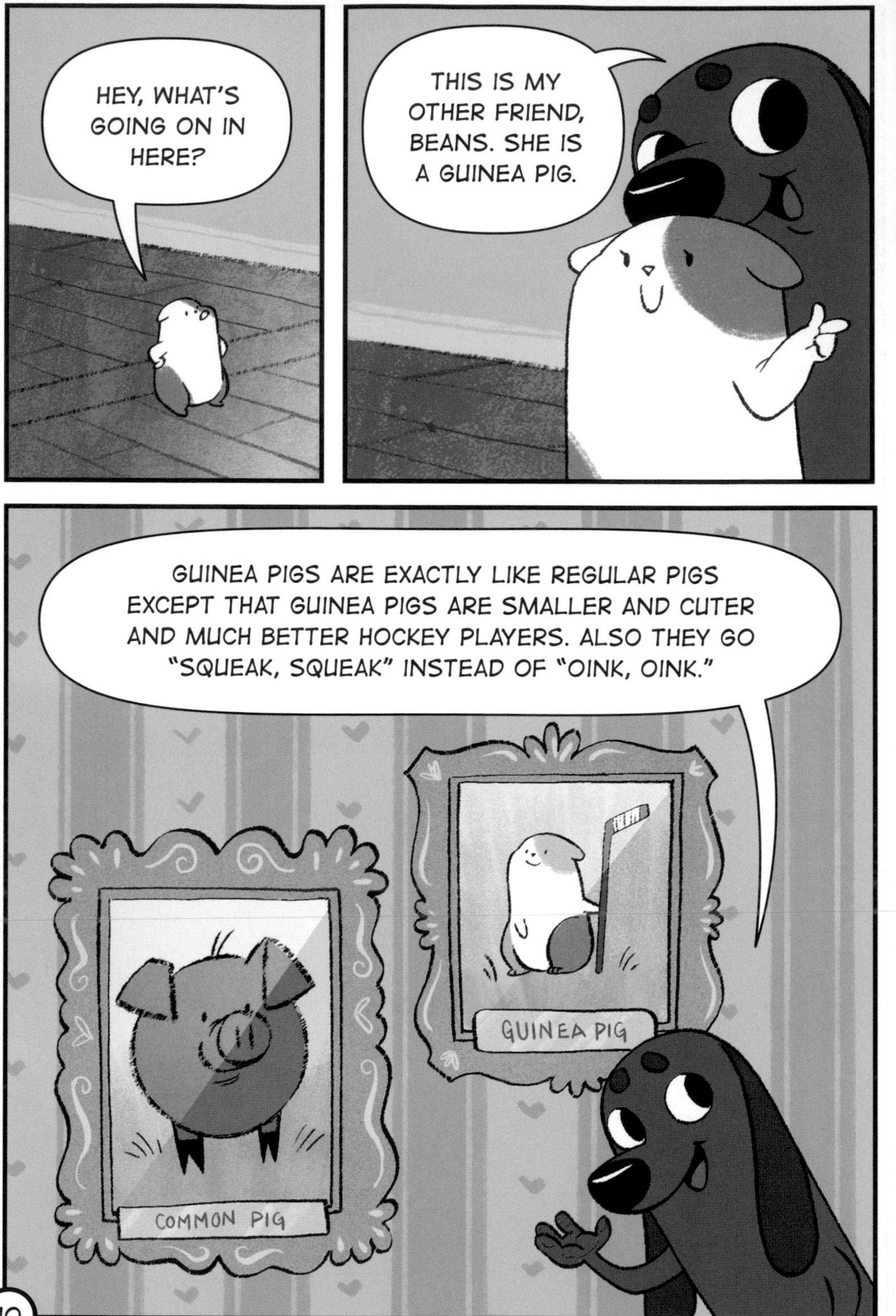
HEY, WHAT'S GOING ON IN HERE?
THIS IS MY OTHER FRIEND, BEANS. SHE IS A GUINEA PIG.
GUINEA PIGS ARE EXACTLY LIKE REGULAR PIGS EXCEPT THAT GUINEA PIGS ARE SMALLER AND CUTER AND MUCH BETTER HOCKEY PLAYERS. ALSO THEY GO "SQUEAK, SQUEAK" INSTEAD OF "OINK, OINK."
COMMON PIG
GUINEA PIG

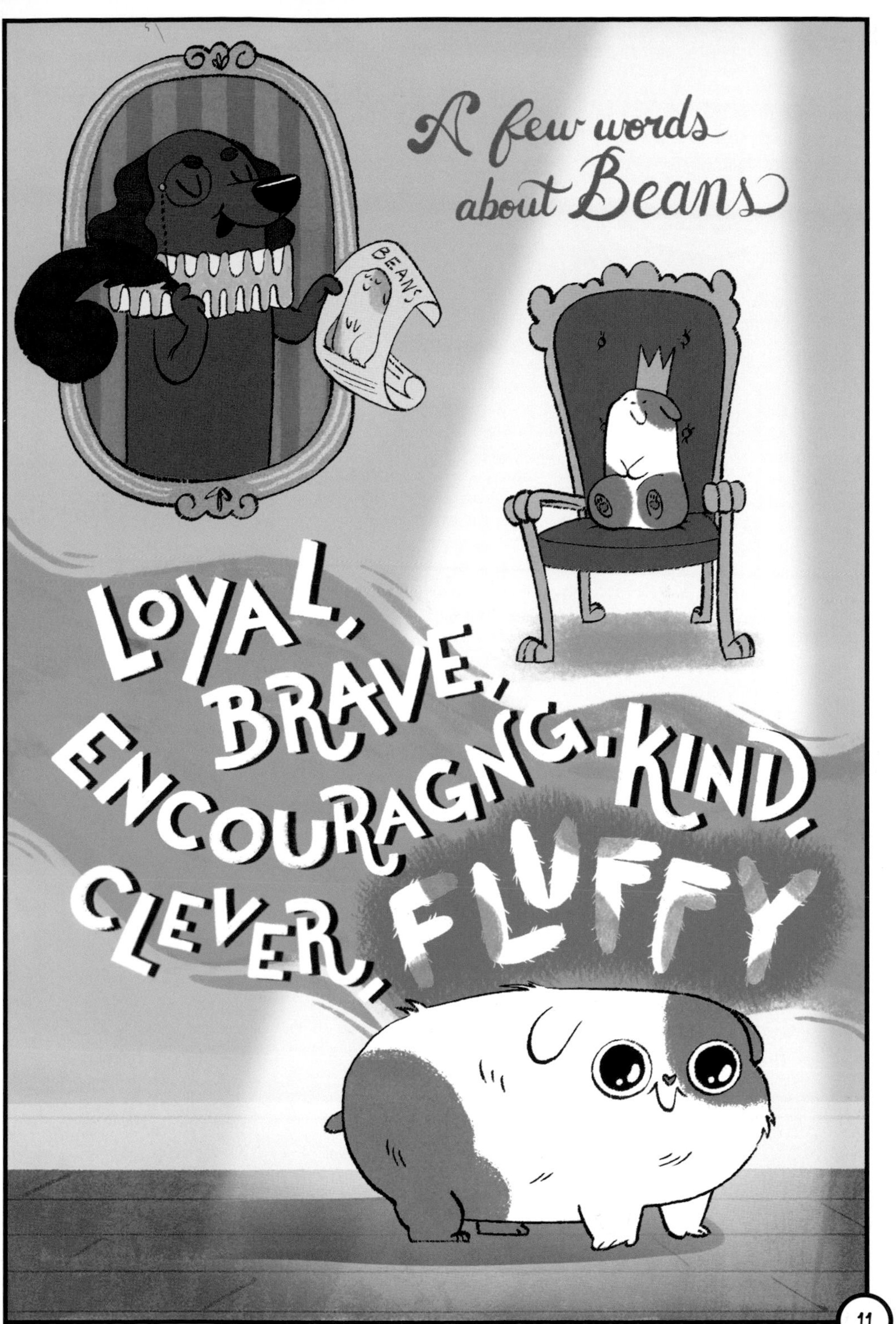

A few words about Beans
BEANS
LOYAL, BRAVE, ENCOURAGNG, KIND, CLEVER, FLUFFY

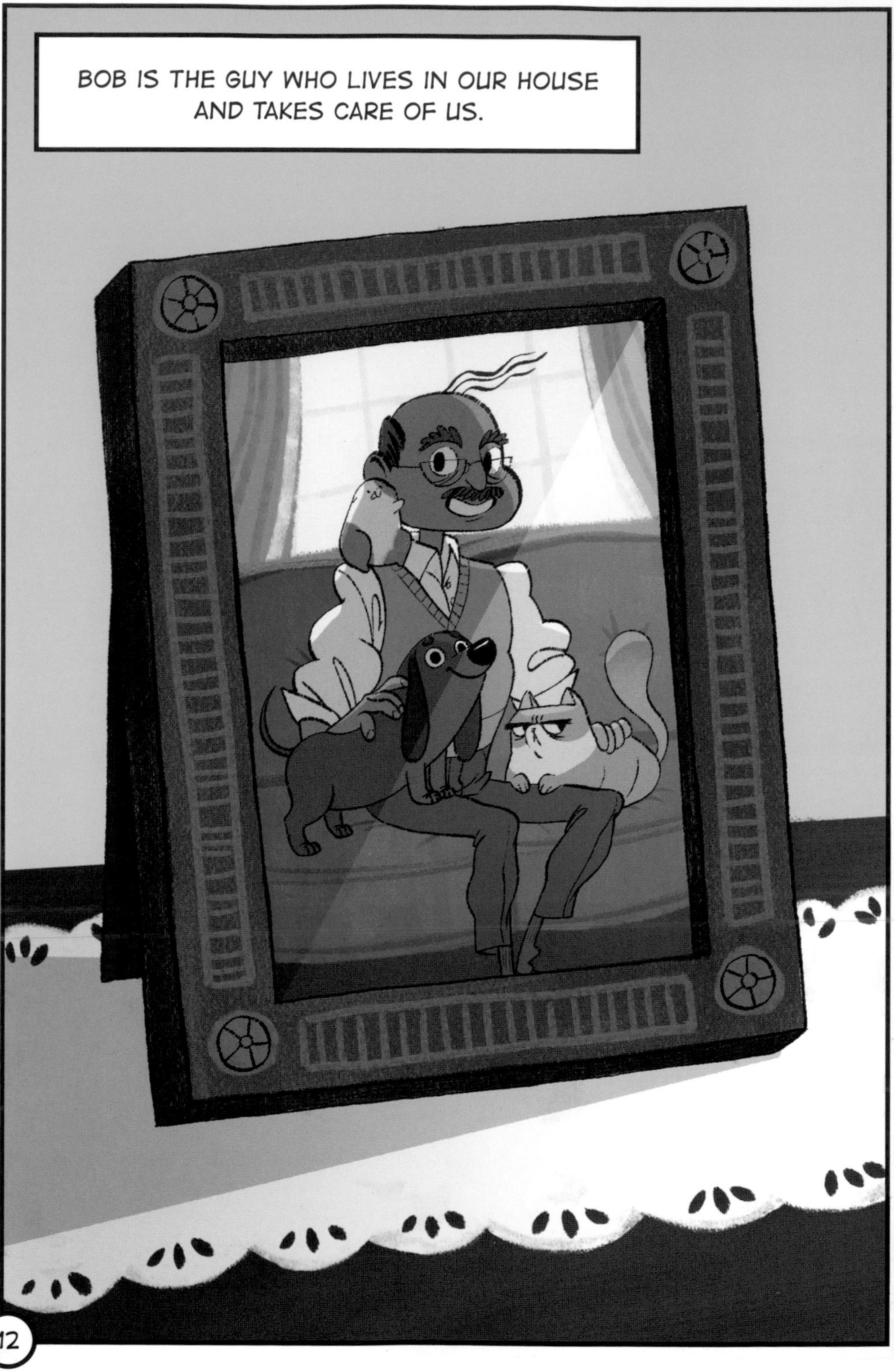
BOB IS THE GUY WHO LIVES IN OUR HOUSE AND TAKES CARE OF US.

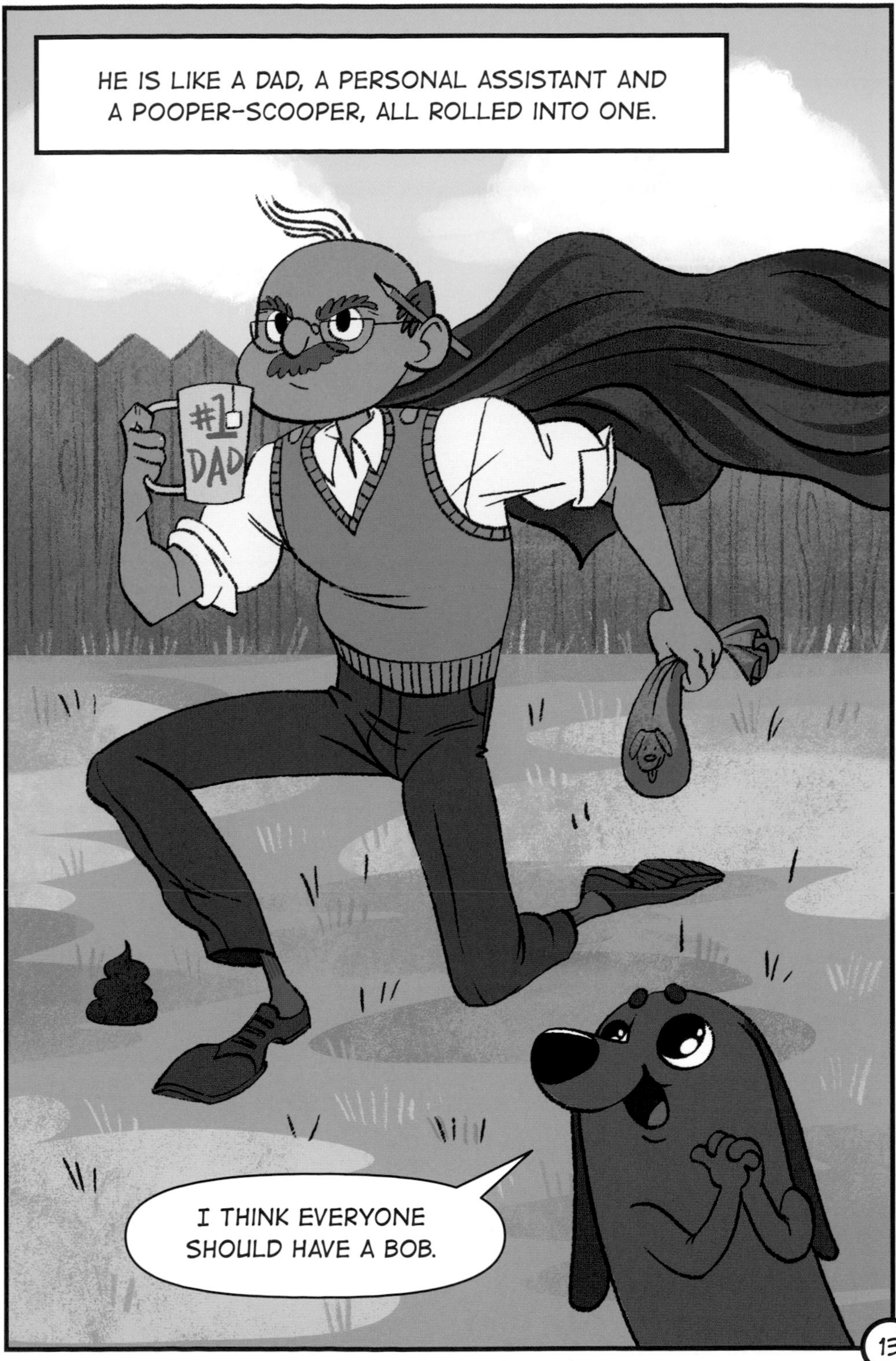
HE IS LIKE A DAD, A PERSONAL ASSISTANT AND A POOPER-SCOOPER, ALL ROLLED INTO ONE.
#1 DAD
I THINK EVERYONE SHOULD HAVE A BOB.

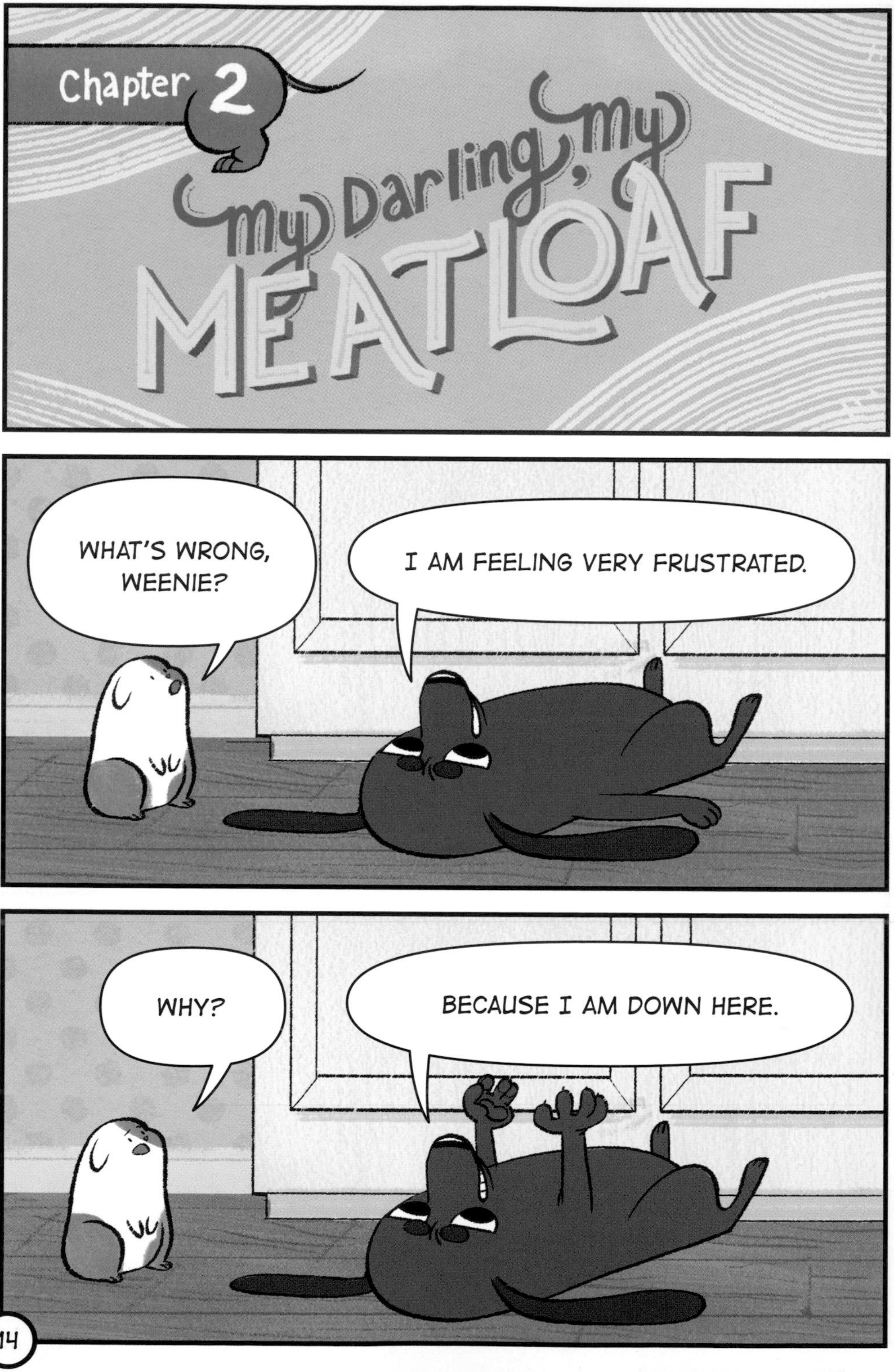

Chapter 2
My Darling, My MEATLOAF
WHAT'S WRONG, WEENIE?
I AM FEELING VERY FRUSTRATED.
WHY?
BECAUSE I AM DOWN HERE.

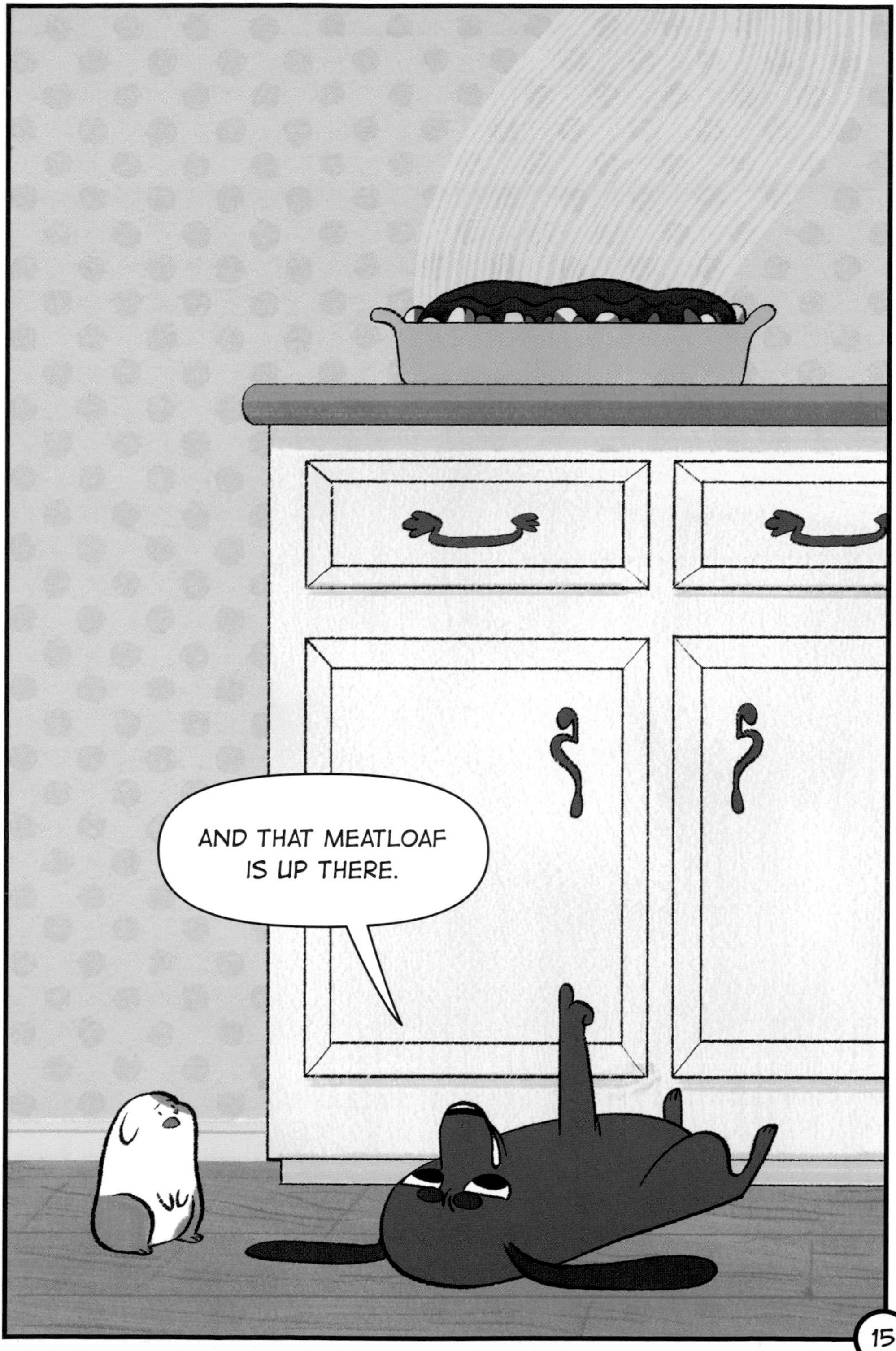
AND THAT MEATLOAF IS UP THERE.

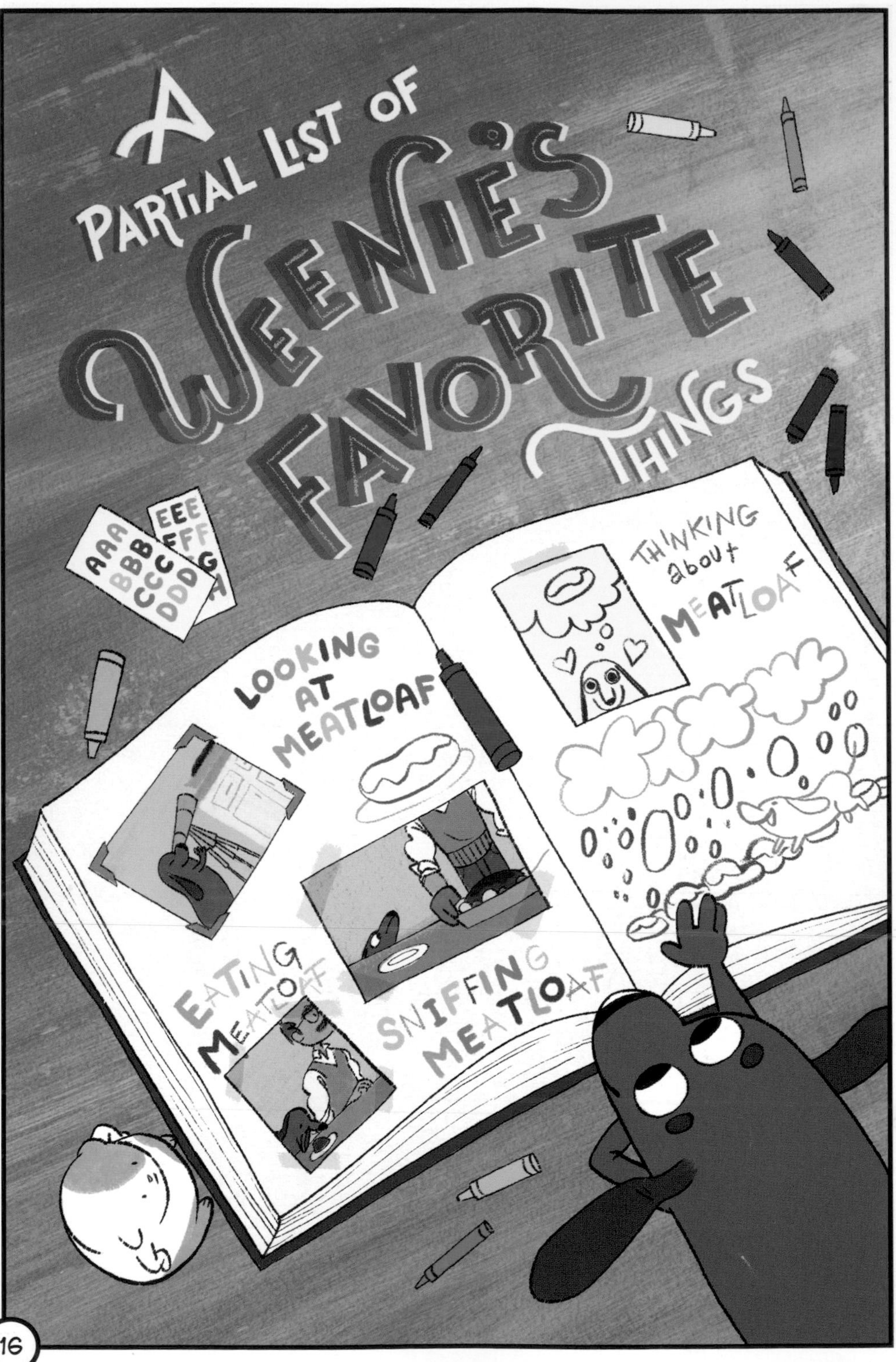
A PARTIAL LIST OF WEENIE'S FAVORITE THINGS
THINKING about MEATLOAF
LOOKING AT MEATLOAF
EATING MEATLOAF
SNIFFING MEATLOAF

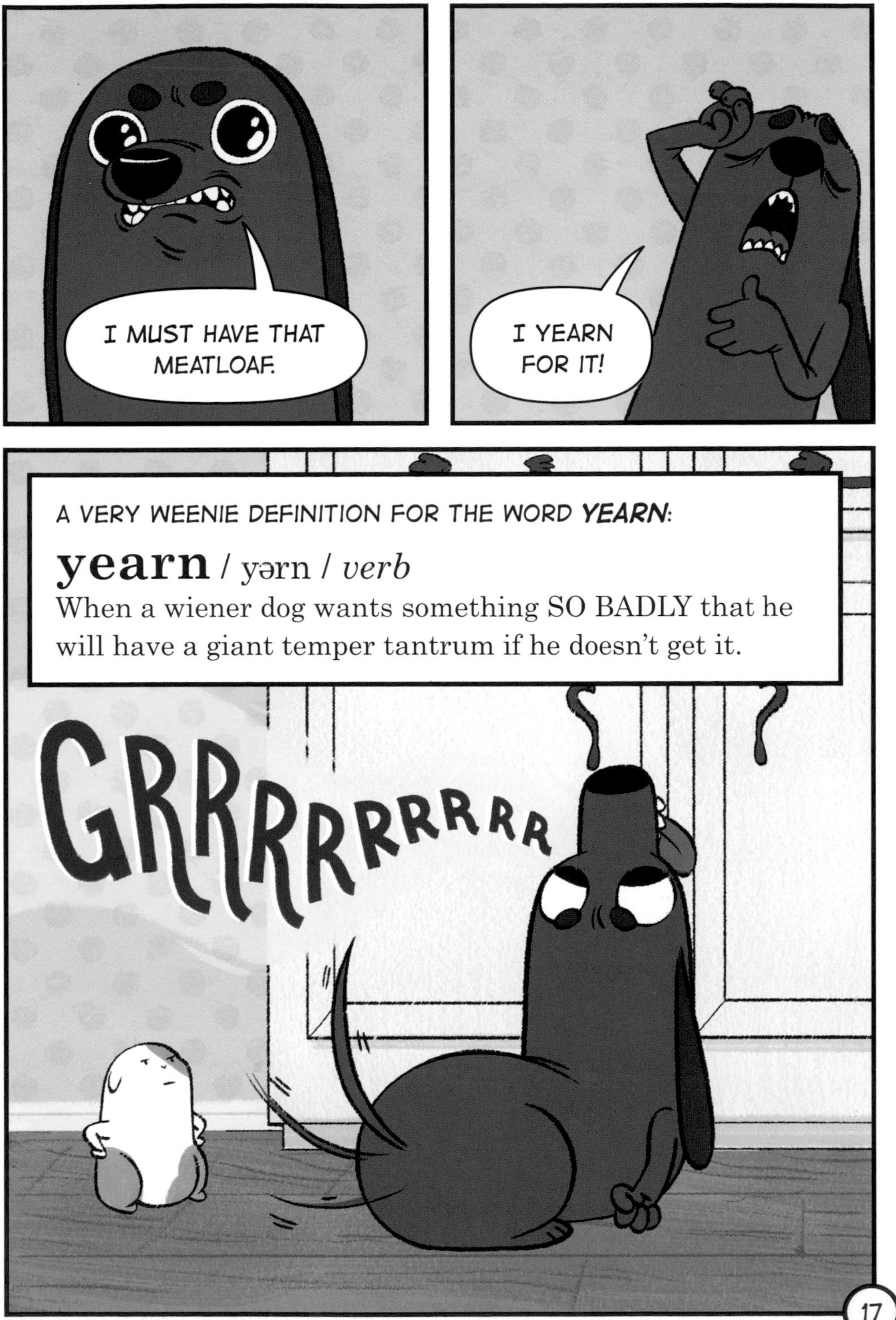

I MUST HAVE THAT MEATLOAF.
I YEARN FOR IT!
A VERY WEENIE DEFINITION FOR THE WORD YEARN:
yearn / yərn / verb
When a wiener dog wants something SO BADLY that he will have a giant temper tantrum if he doesn't get it.
GRRRRRRRRR

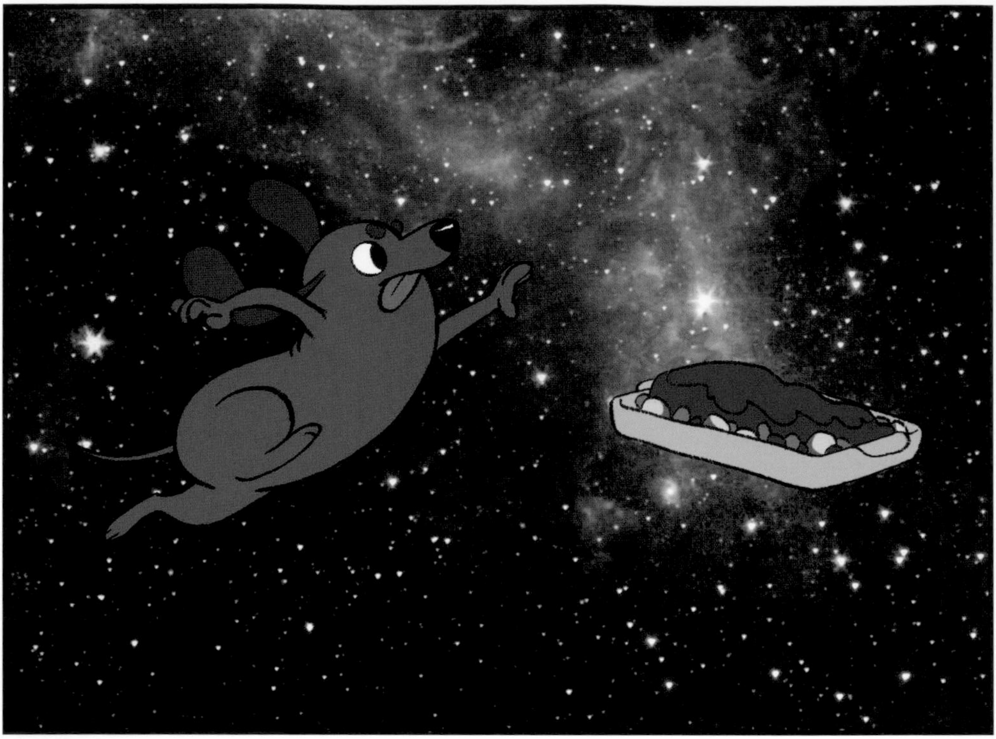

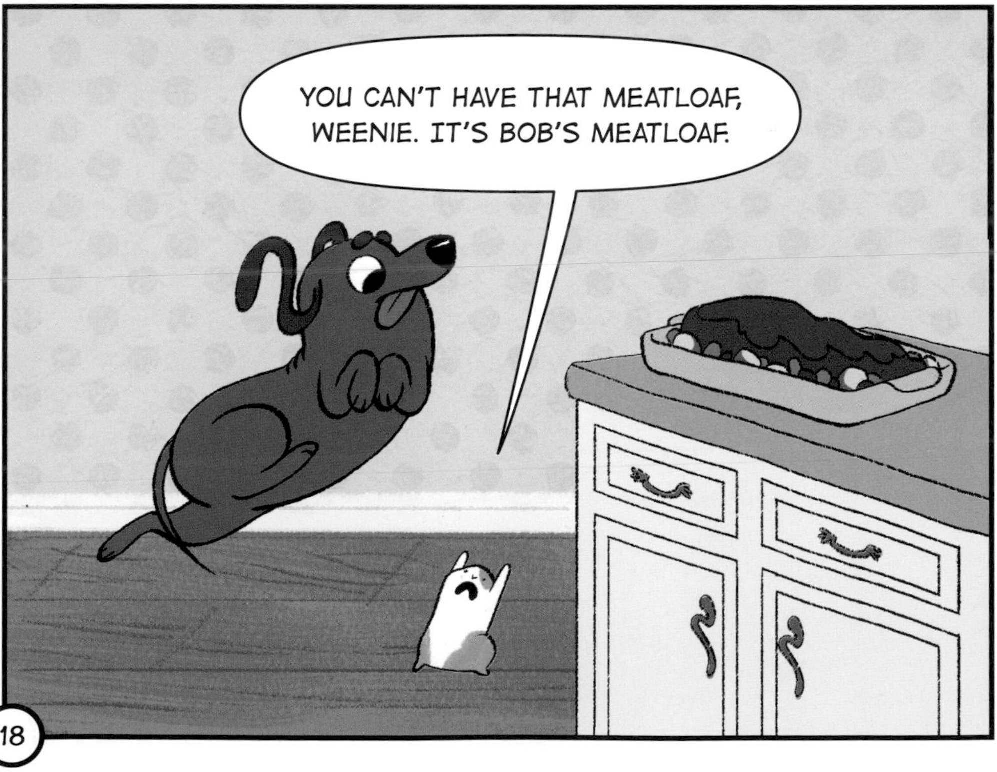
YOU CAN'T HAVE THAT MEATLOAF, WEENIE. IT'S BOB'S MEATLOAF.

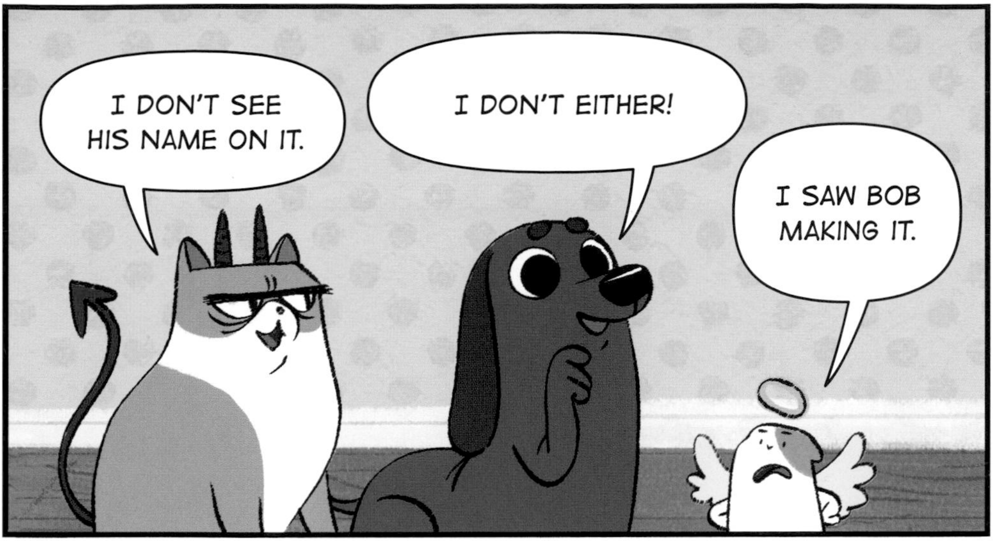
I DON'T SEE HIS NAME ON IT.
I DON'T EITHER!
I SAW BOB MAKING IT.

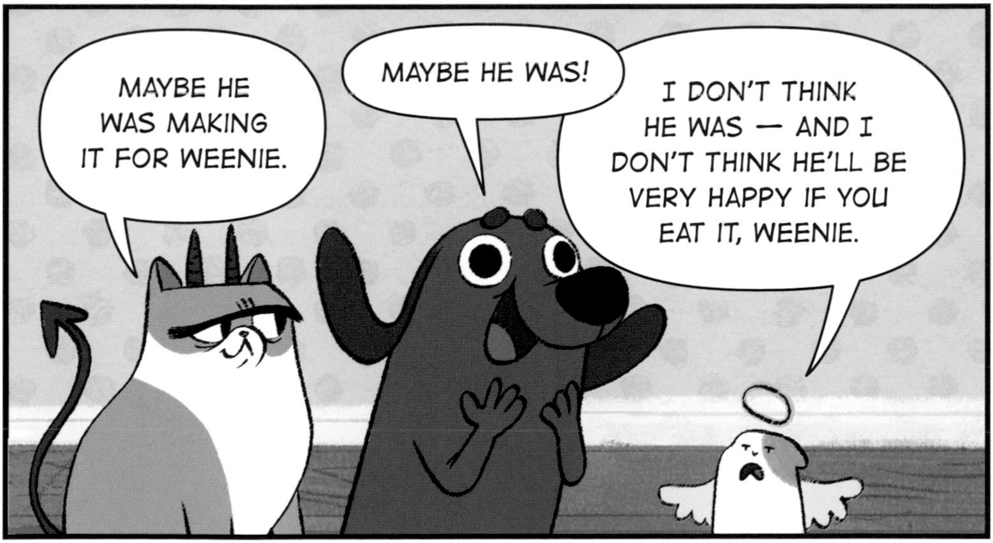
MAYBE HE WAS MAKING IT FOR WEENIE.
MAYBE HE WAS!
I DON'T THINK HE WAS — AND I DON'T THINK HE'LL BE VERY HAPPY IF YOU EAT IT, WEENIE.

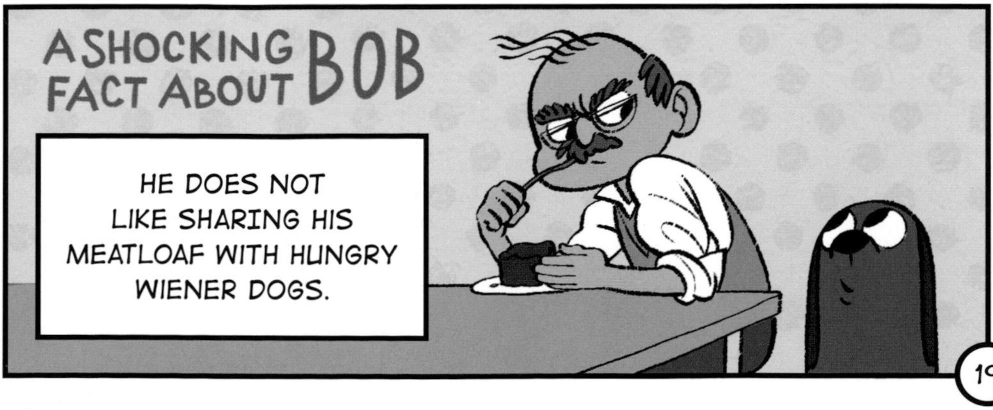
A SHOCKING FACT ABOUT BOB
HE DOES NOT LIKE SHARING HIS MEATLOAF WITH HUNGRY WIENER DOGS.

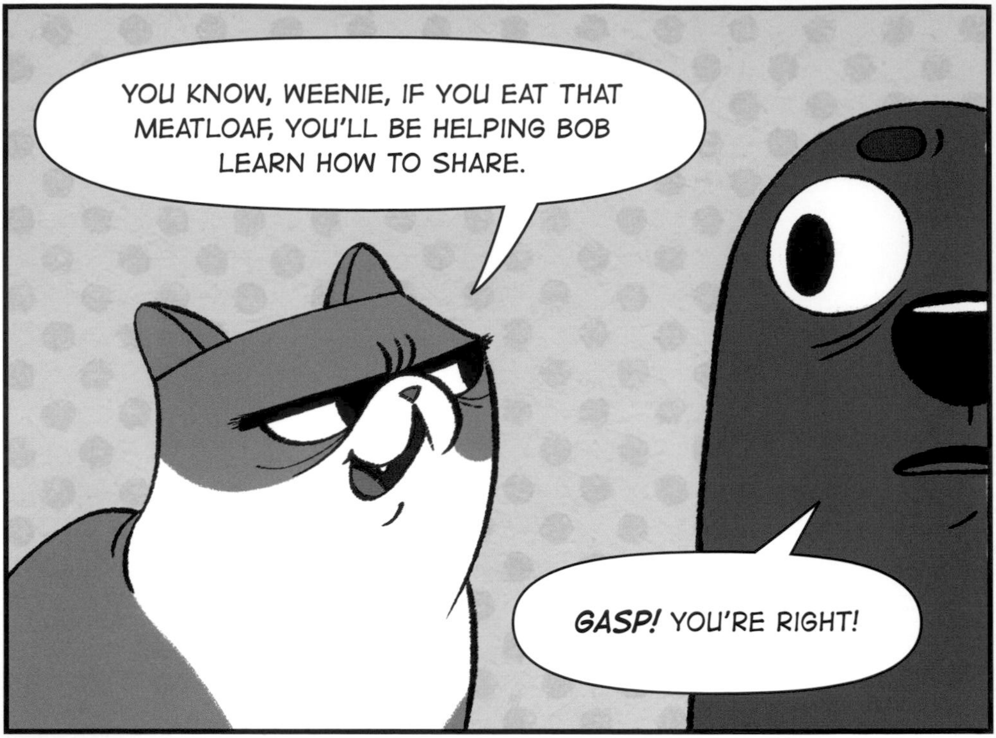
YOU KNOW, WEENIE, IF YOU EAT THAT MEATLOAF, YOU'LL BE HELPING BOB LEARN HOW TO SHARE.
GASP! YOU'RE RIGHT!

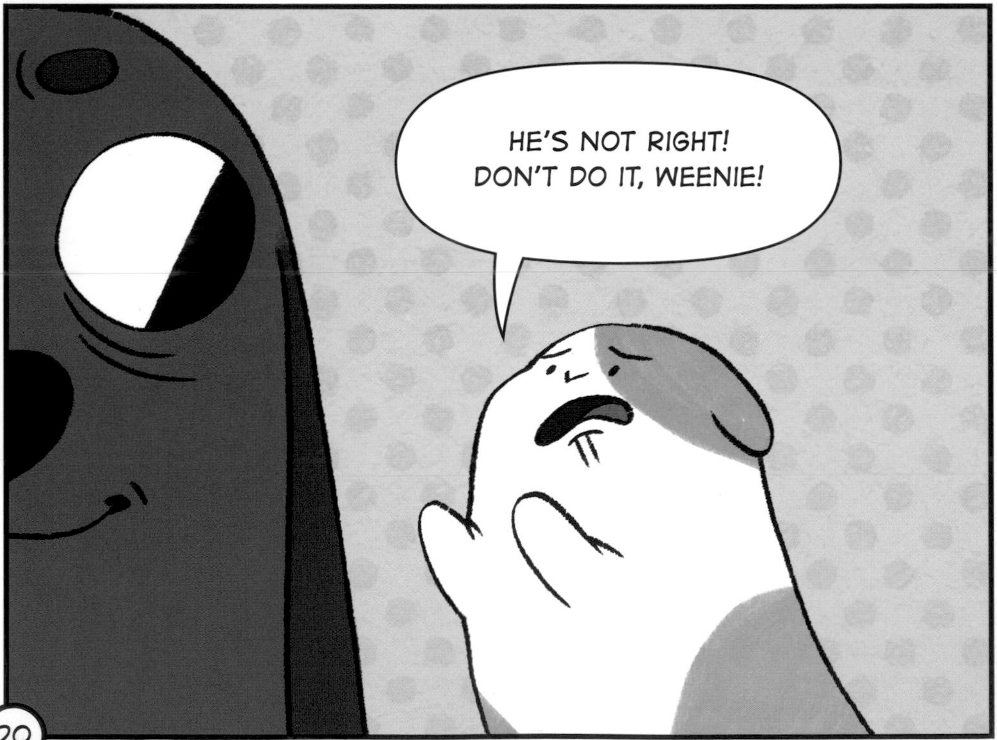
HE'S NOT RIGHT! DON'T DO IT, WEENIE!

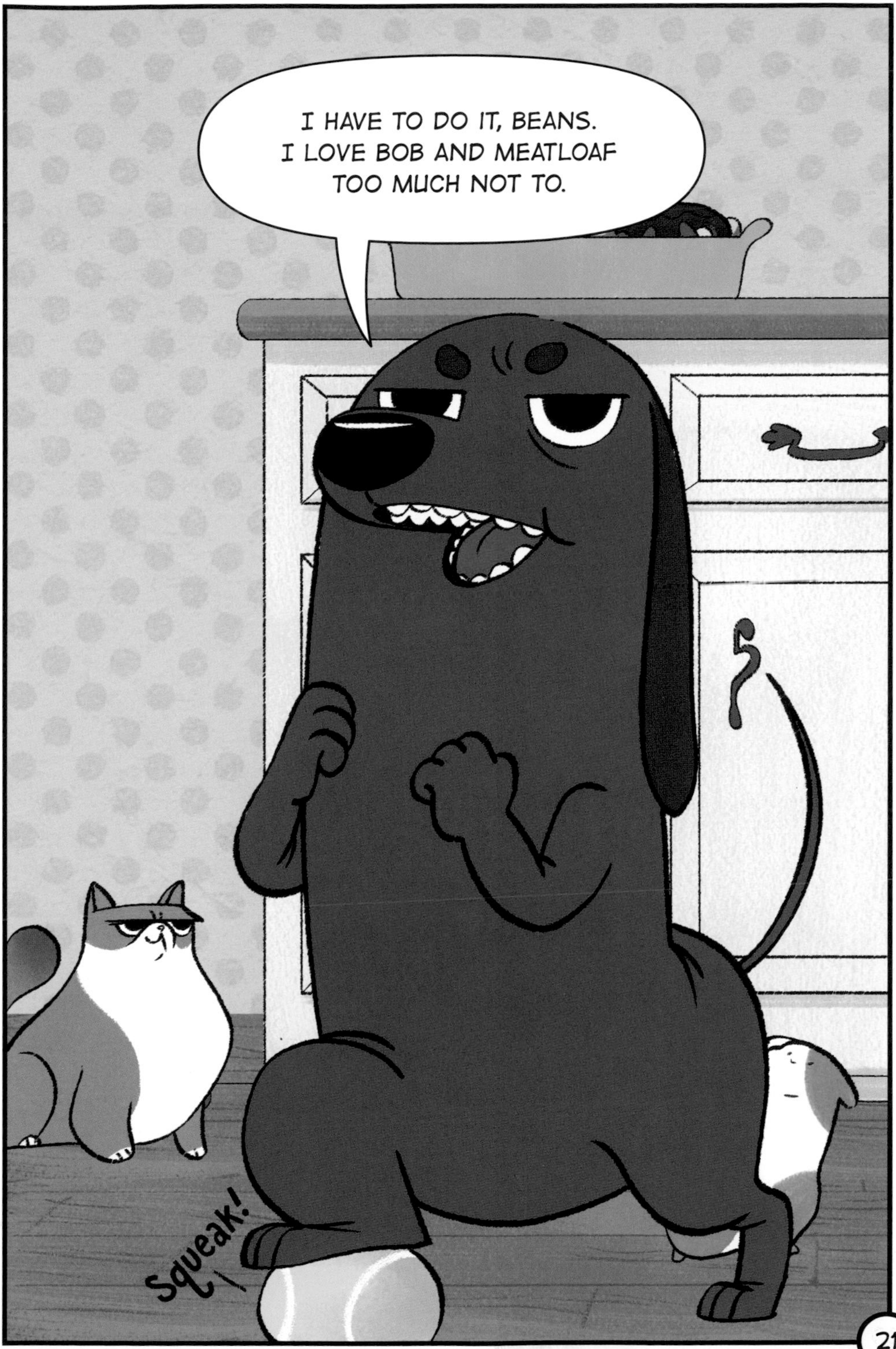
I HAVE TO DO IT, BEANS. I LOVE BOB AND MEATLOAF TOO MUCH NOT TO.
Squeak!

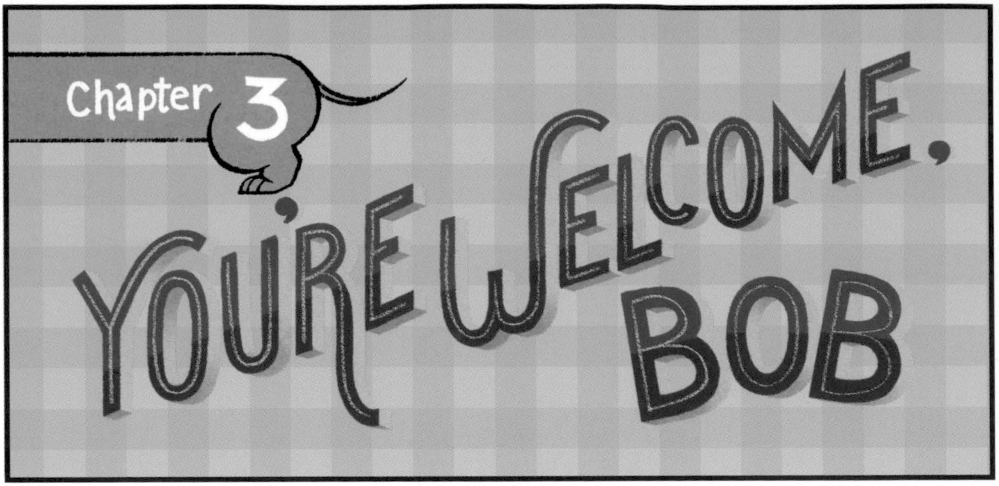
Chapter 3
YOU'RE WELCOME, BOB

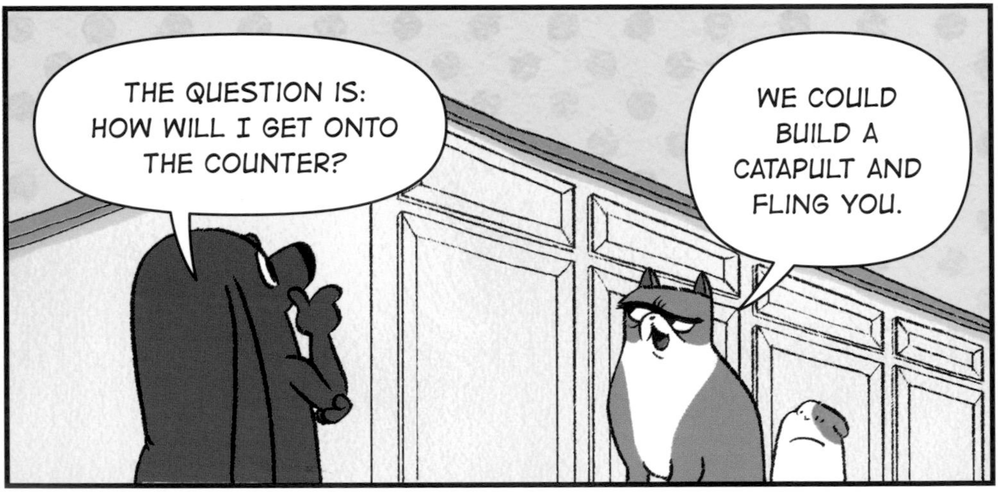
THE QUESTION IS: HOW WILL I GET ONTO THE COUNTER?
WE COULD BUILD A CATAPULT AND FLING YOU.

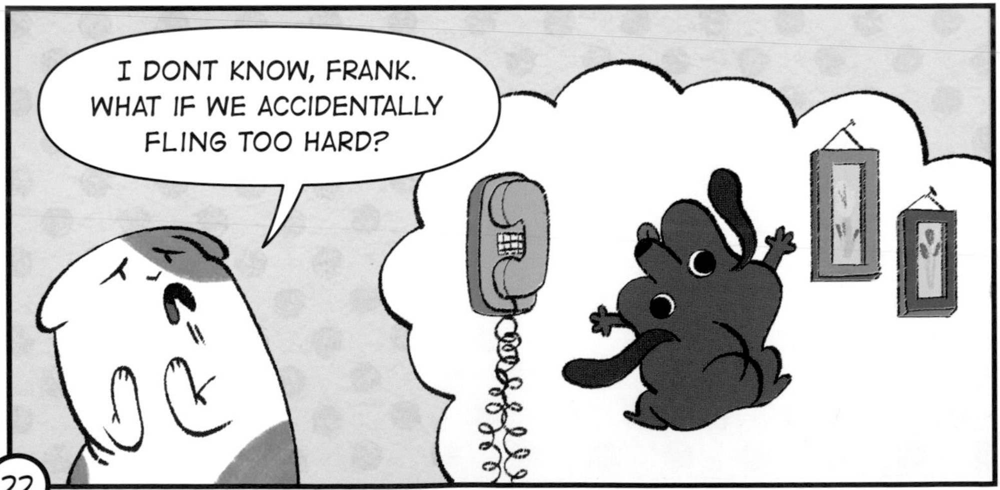
I DONT KNOW, FRANK. WHAT IF WE ACCIDENTALLY FLING TOO HARD?

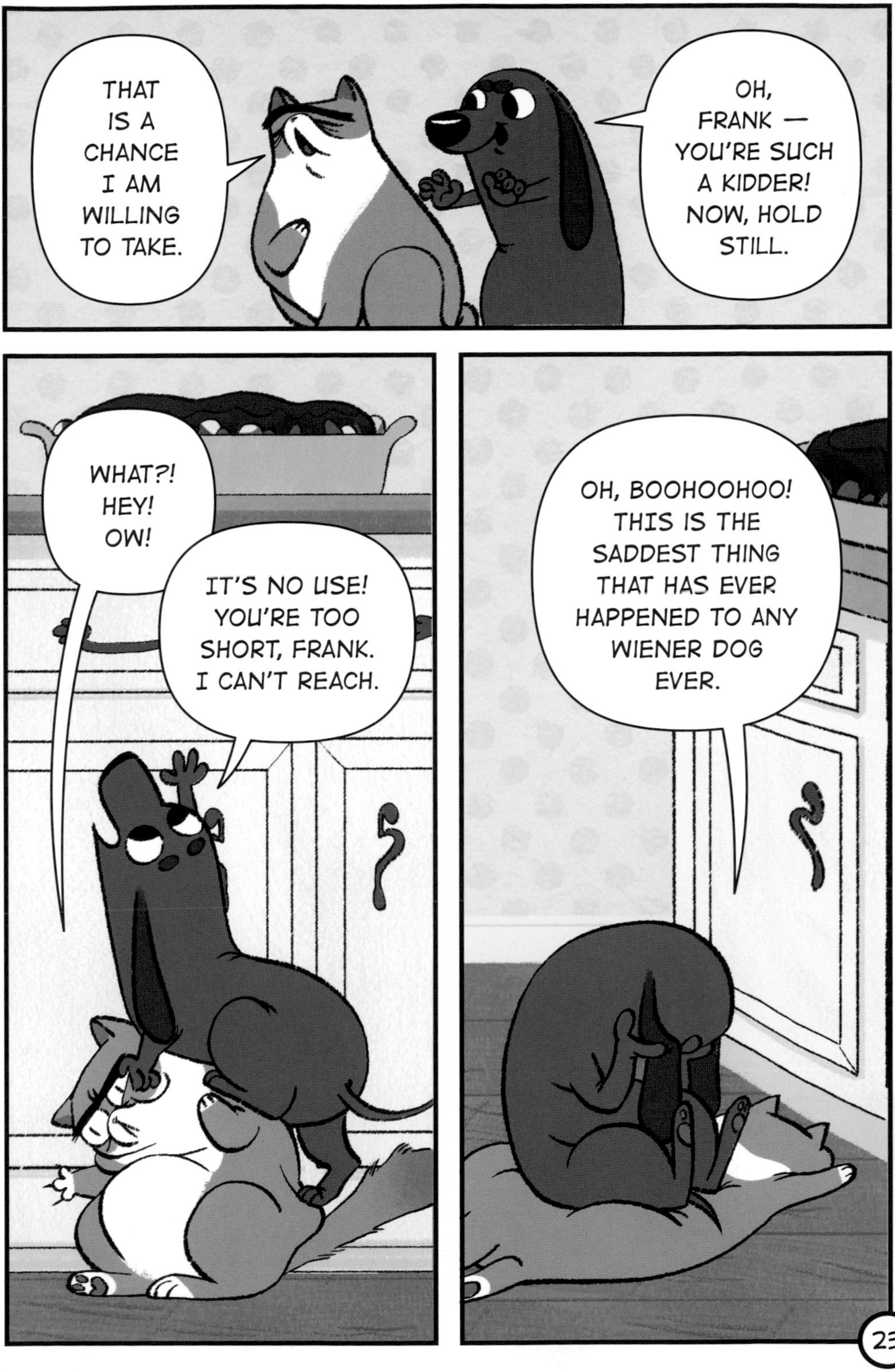
THAT IS A CHANCE I AM WILLING TO TAKE.
OH, FRANK — YOU'RE SUCH A KIDDER! NOW, HOLD STILL.
WHAT?! HEY! OW!
IT'S NO USE! YOU'RE TOO SHORT, FRANK. I CAN'T REACH.
OH, BOOHOOHOO! THIS IS THE SADDEST THING THAT HAS EVER HAPPENED TO ANY WIENER DOG EVER.

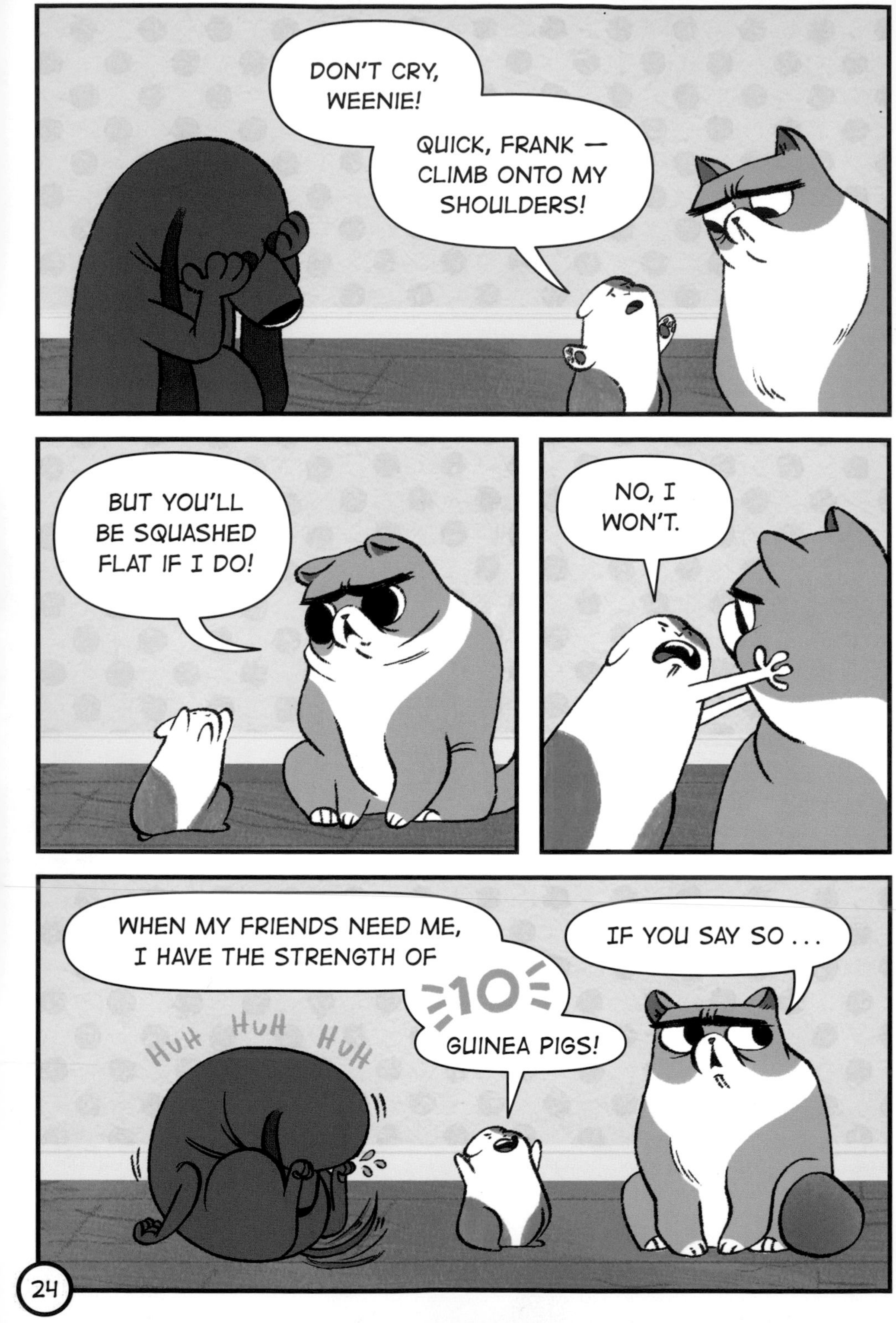
DON'T CRY, WEENIE!
QUICK, FRANK — CLIMB ONTO MY SHOULDERS!
BUT YOU'LL BE SQUASHED FLAT IF I DO!
NO, I WON'T.
WHEN MY FRIENDS NEED ME, I HAVE THE STRENGTH OF 10 GUINEA PIGS!
IF YOU SAY SO . . .
HUH HUH HUH

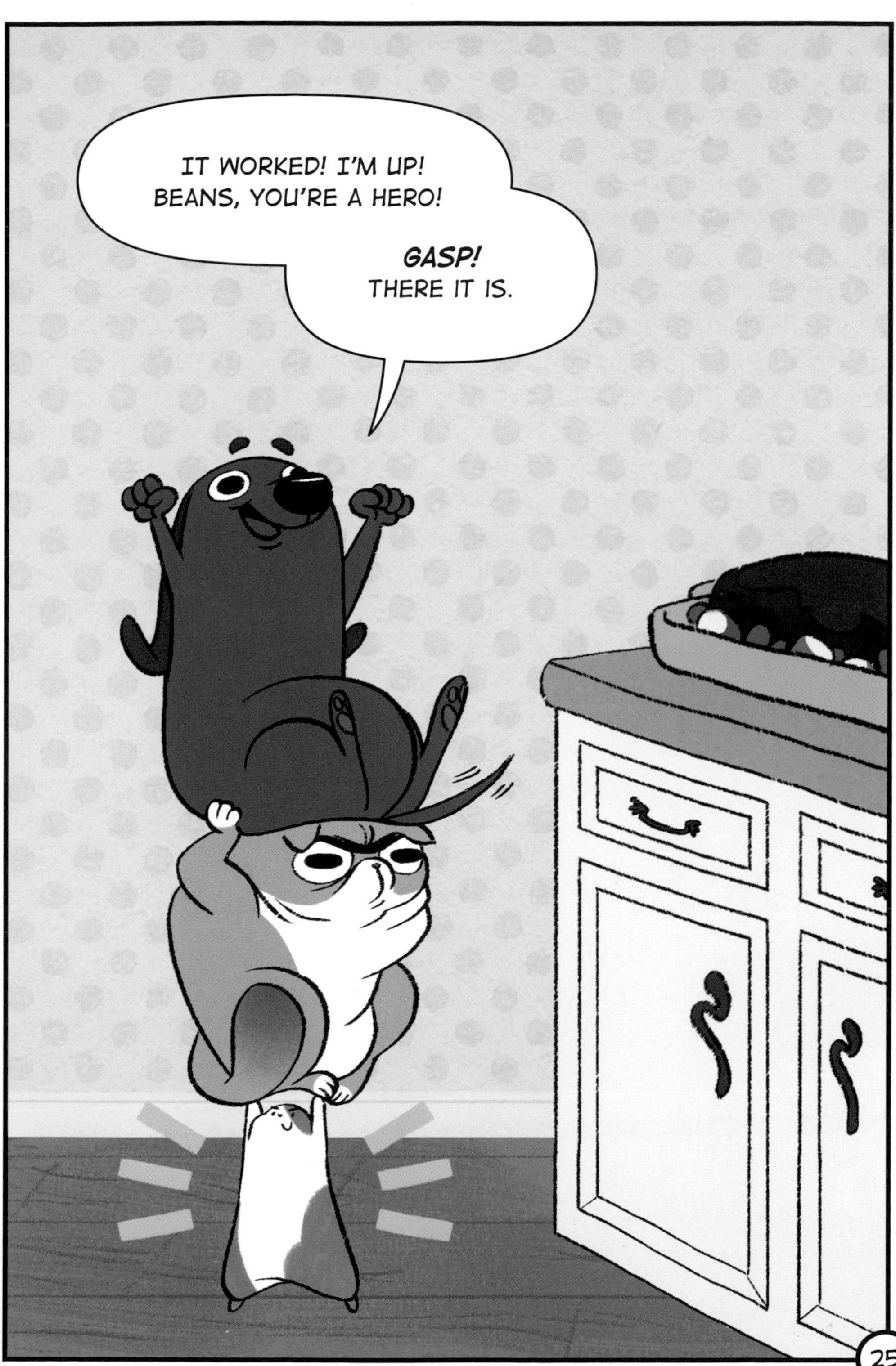
IT WORKED! I'M UP!
BEANS, YOU'RE A HERO!
GASP!
THERE IT IS.

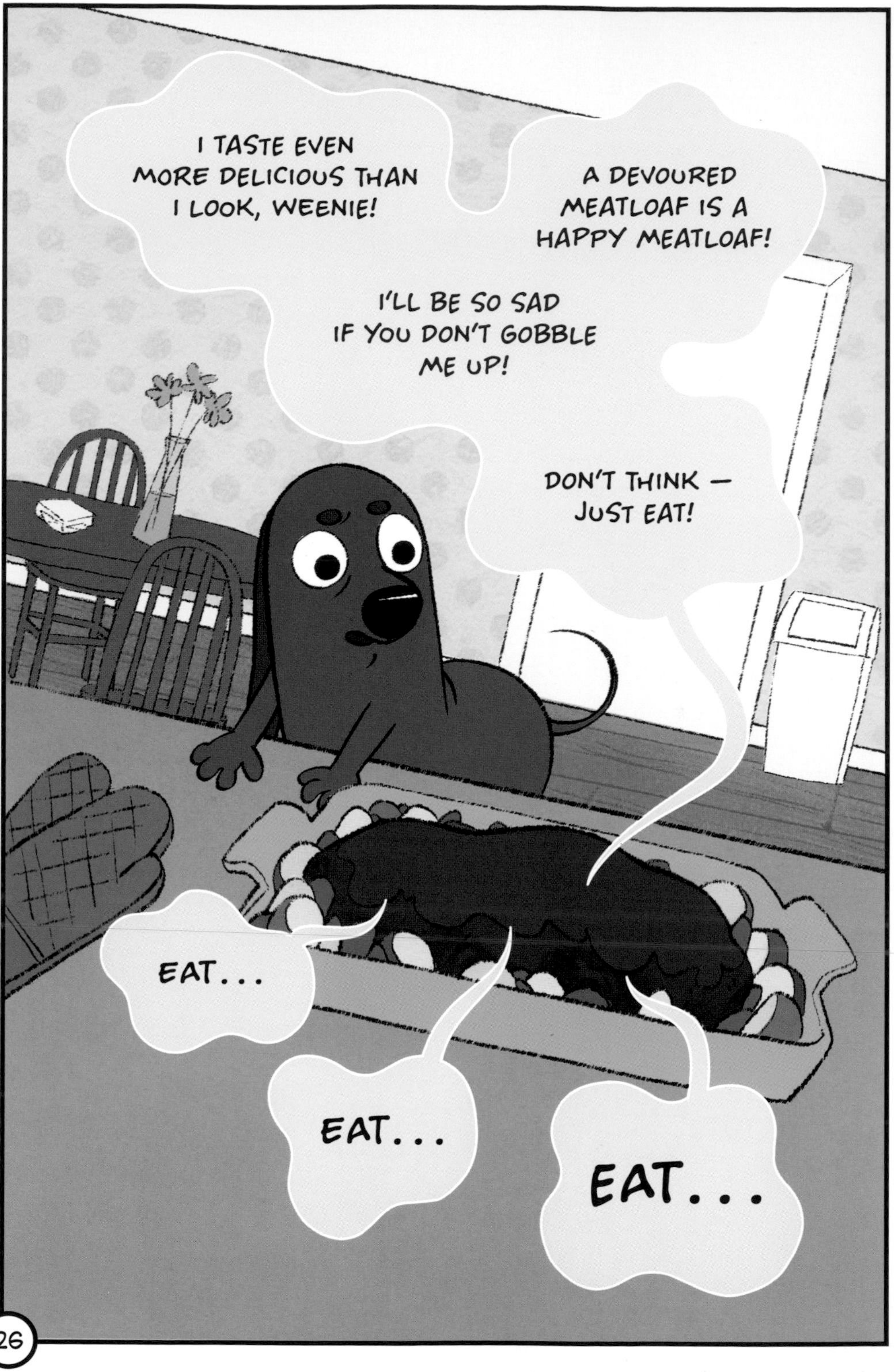
I TASTE EVEN MORE DELICIOUS THAN I LOOK, WEENIE!
A DEVOURED MEATLOAF IS A HAPPY MEATLOAF!
I'LL BE SO SAD IF YOU DON'T GOBBLE ME UP!
DON'T THINK — JUST EAT!
EAT...
EAT...
EAT...

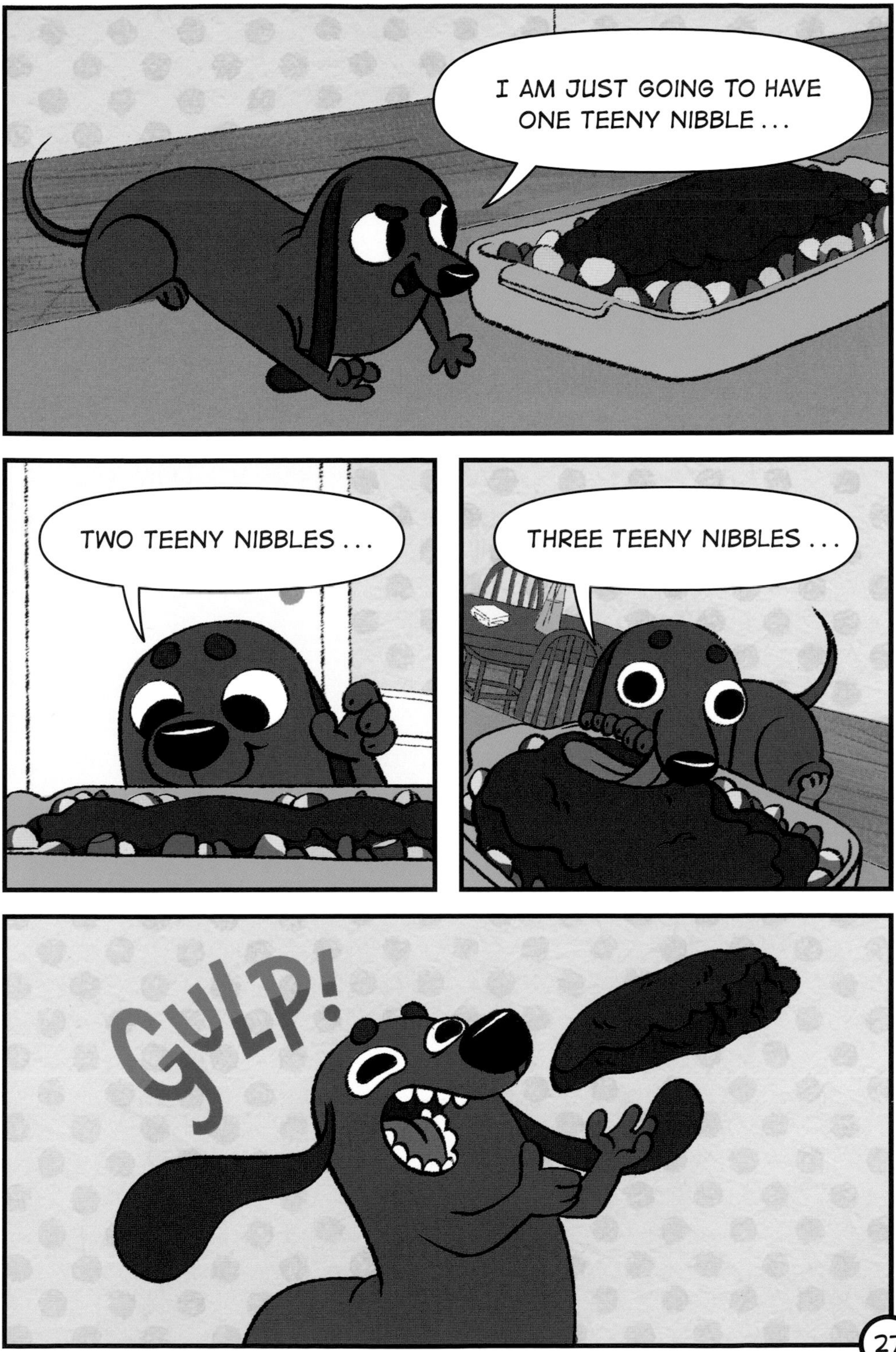
I AM JUST GOING TO HAVE ONE TEENY NIBBLE . . .
TWO TEENY NIBBLES . . .
THREE TEENY NIBBLES . . .
GULP!

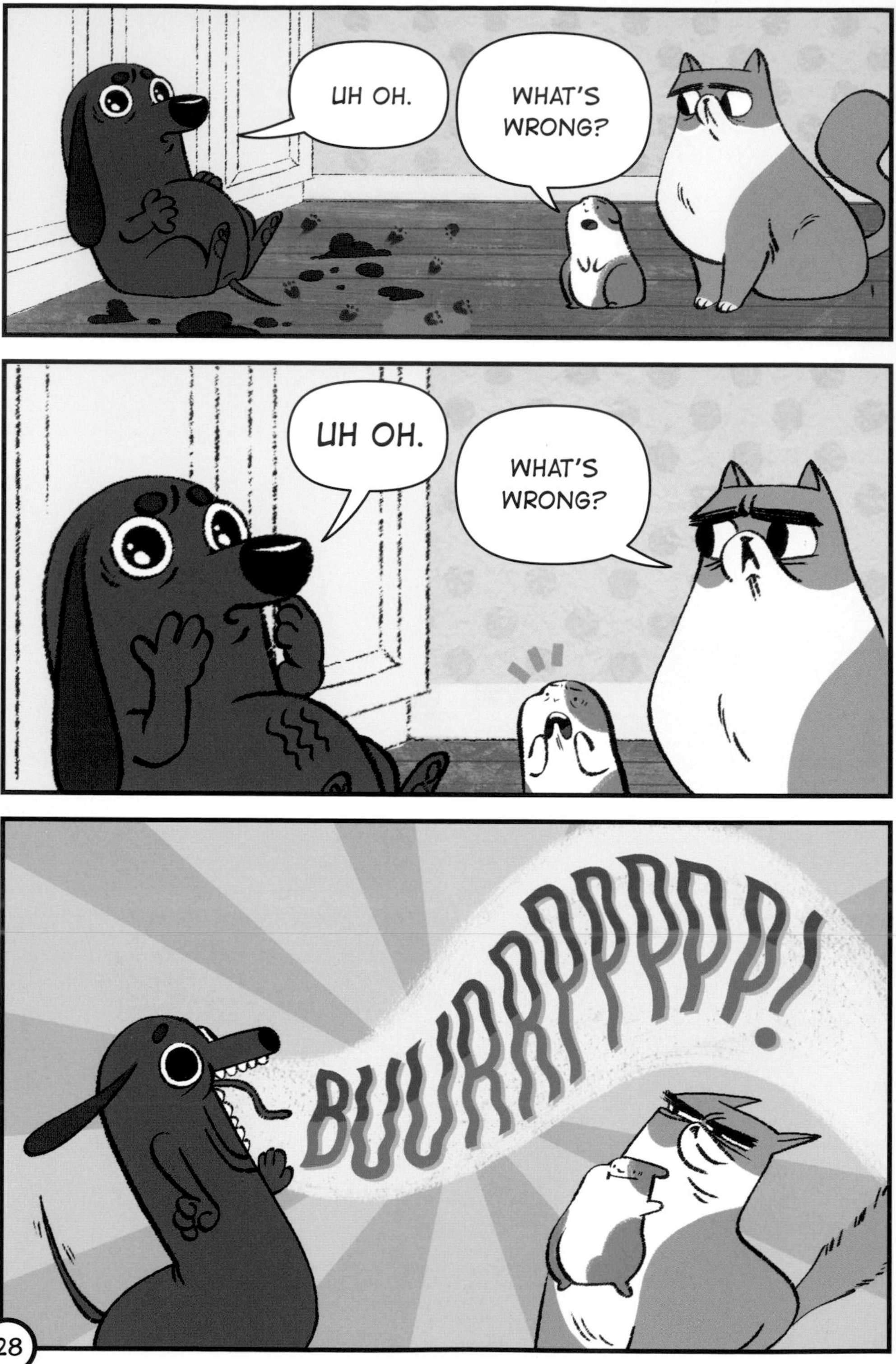
UH OH.
WHAT'S WRONG?
UH OH.
WHAT'S WRONG?
BUURRPPPPP!

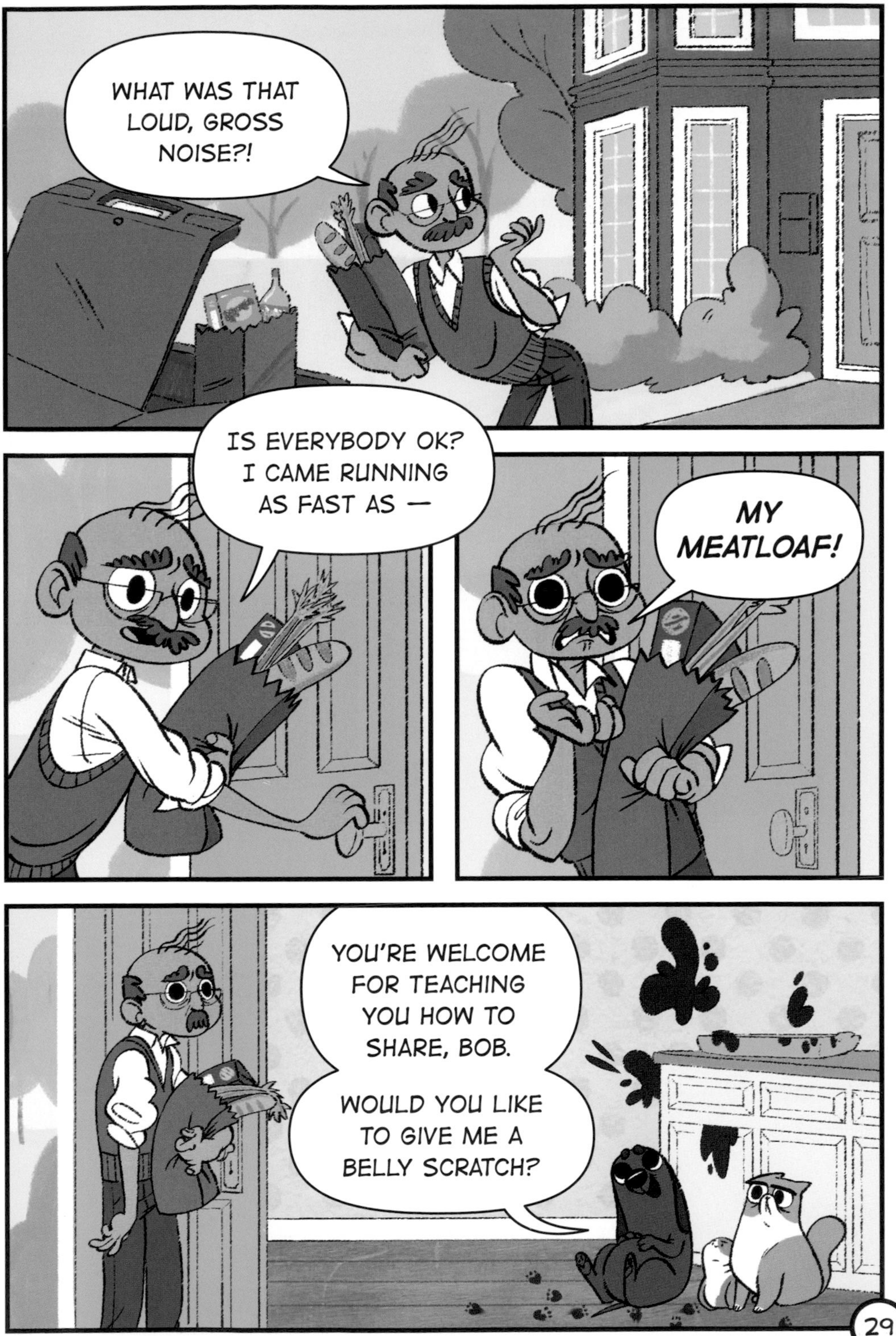
WHAT WAS THAT LOUD, GROSS NOISE?!
IS EVERYBODY OK? I CAME RUNNING AS FAST AS —
MY MEATLOAF!
YOU'RE WELCOME FOR TEACHING YOU HOW TO SHARE, BOB.
WOULD YOU LIKE TO GIVE ME A BELLY SCRATCH?

Chapter 4
MORTAL ENEMY IN AISLE THREE

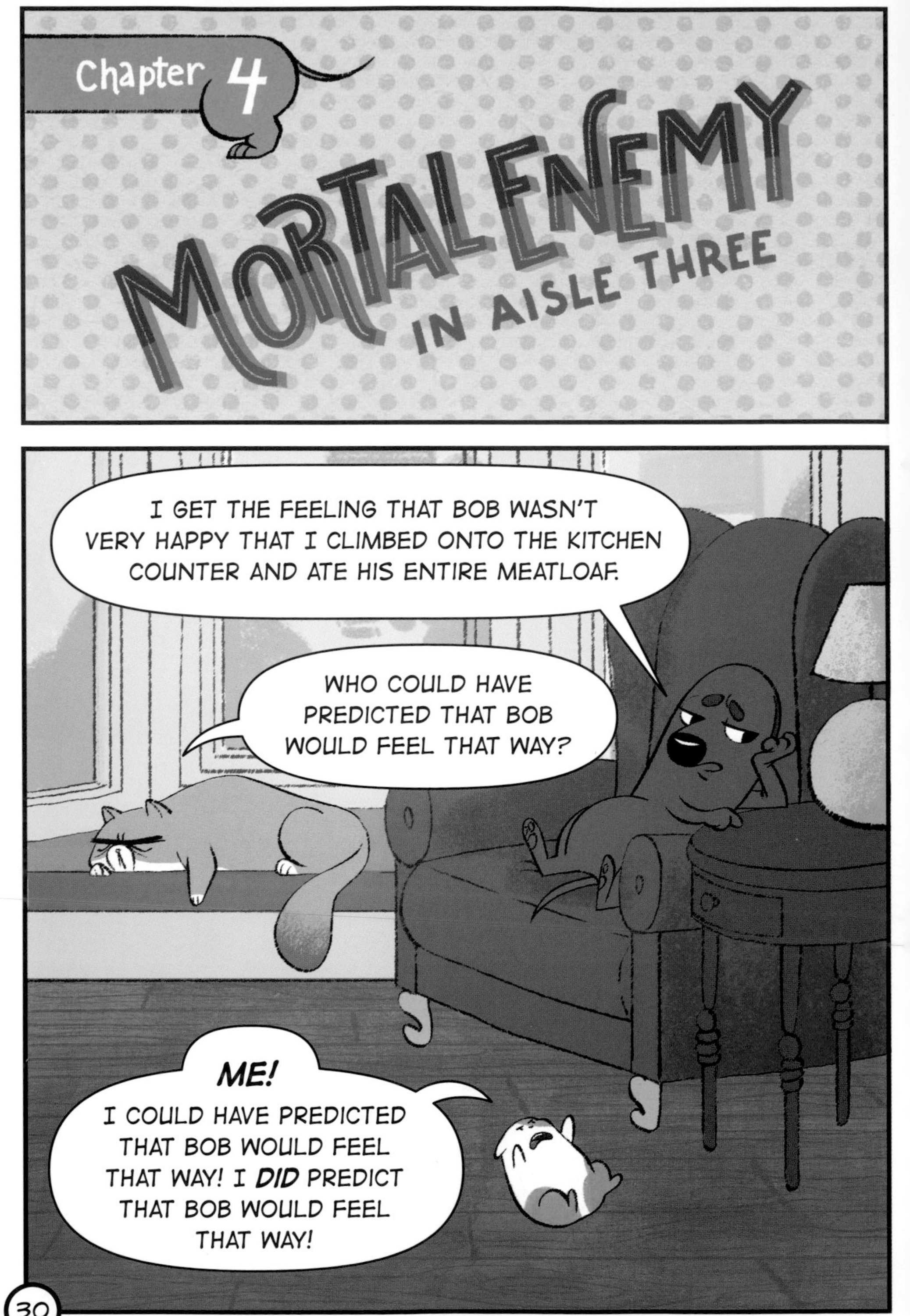
I GET THE FEELING THAT BOB WASN'T VERY HAPPY THAT I CLIMBED ONTO THE KITCHEN COUNTER AND ATE HIS ENTIRE MEATLOAF.
WHO COULD HAVE PREDICTED THAT BOB WOULD FEEL THAT WAY?
ME!
I COULD HAVE PREDICTED THAT BOB WOULD FEEL THAT WAY! I DID PREDICT THAT BOB WOULD FEEL THAT WAY!

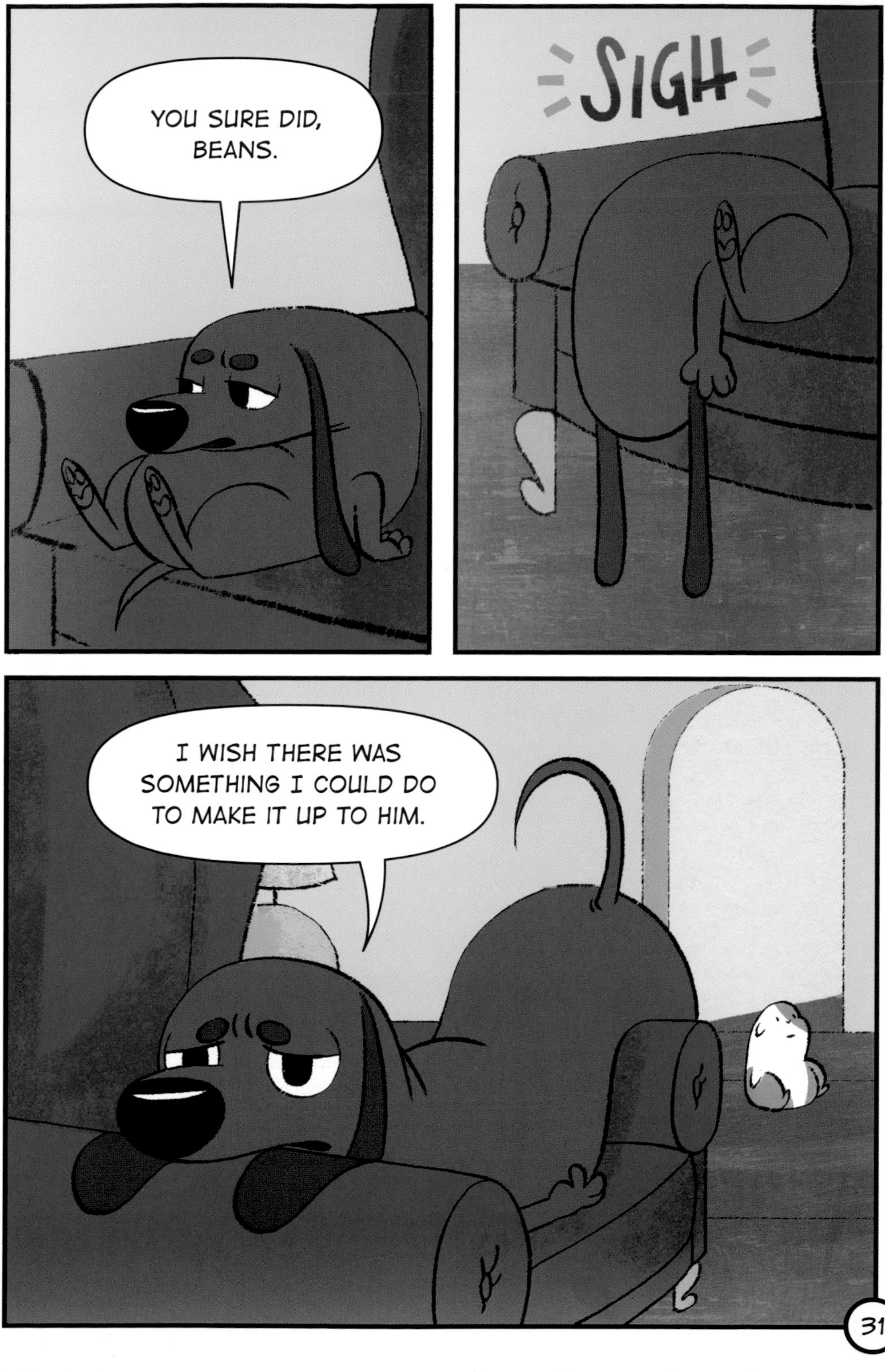
YOU SURE DID, BEANS.
SIGH
I WISH THERE WAS SOMETHING I COULD DO TO MAKE IT UP TO HIM.

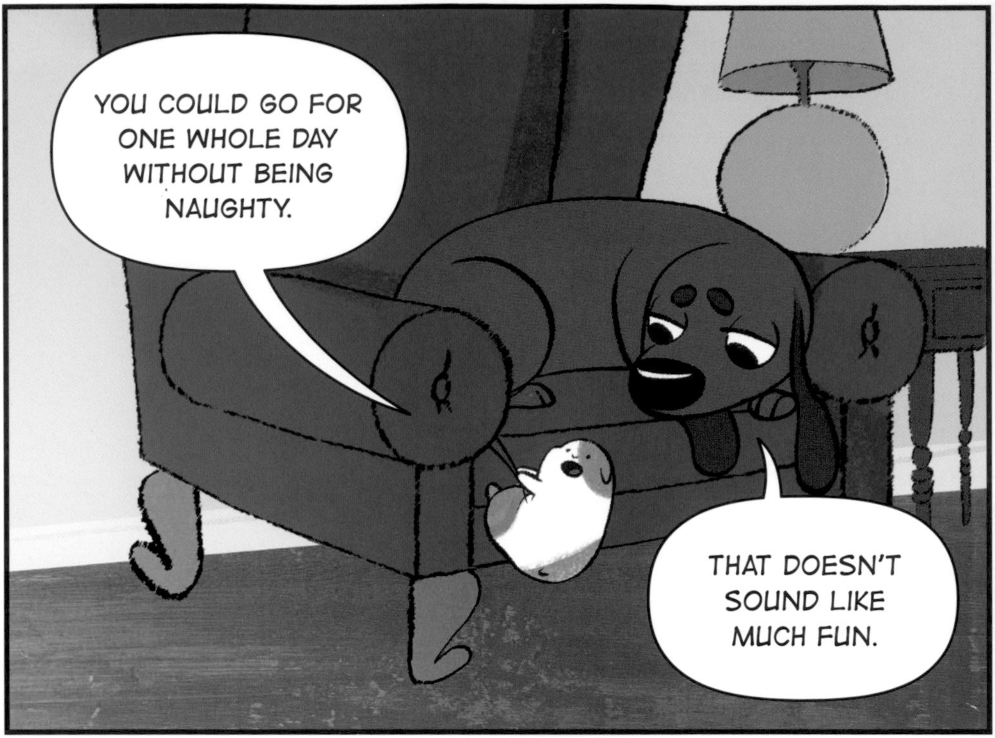
YOU COULD GO FOR ONE WHOLE DAY WITHOUT BEING NAUGHTY.
THAT DOESN'T SOUND LIKE MUCH FUN.

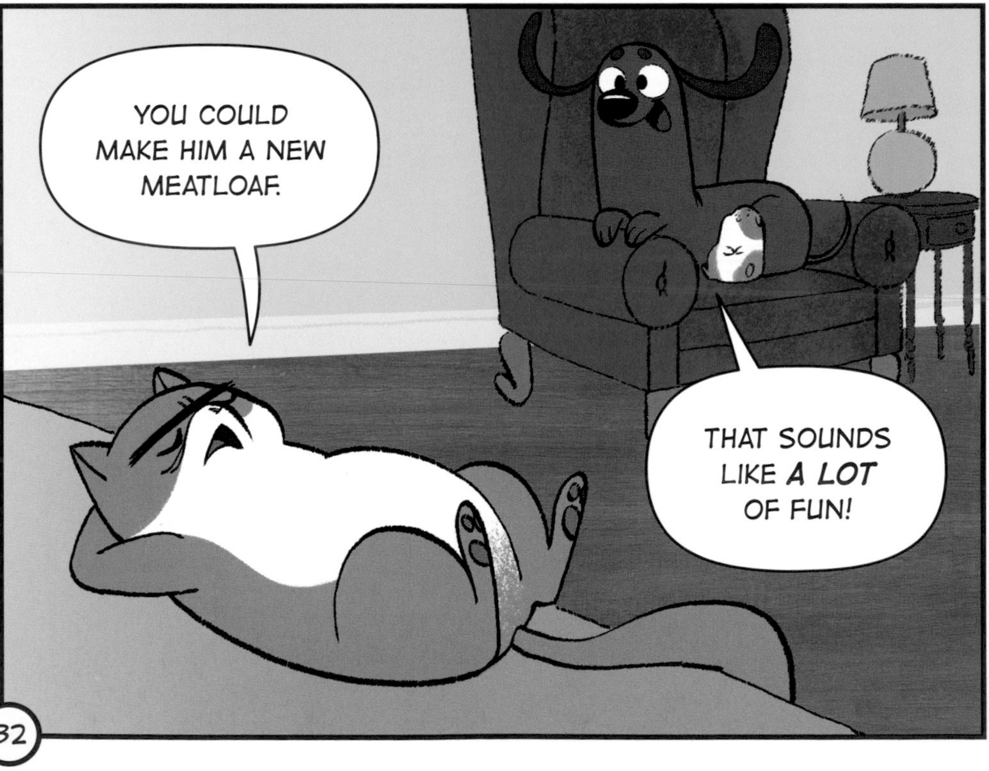
YOU COULD MAKE HIM A NEW MEATLOAF.
THAT SOUNDS LIKE *A LOT* OF FUN!

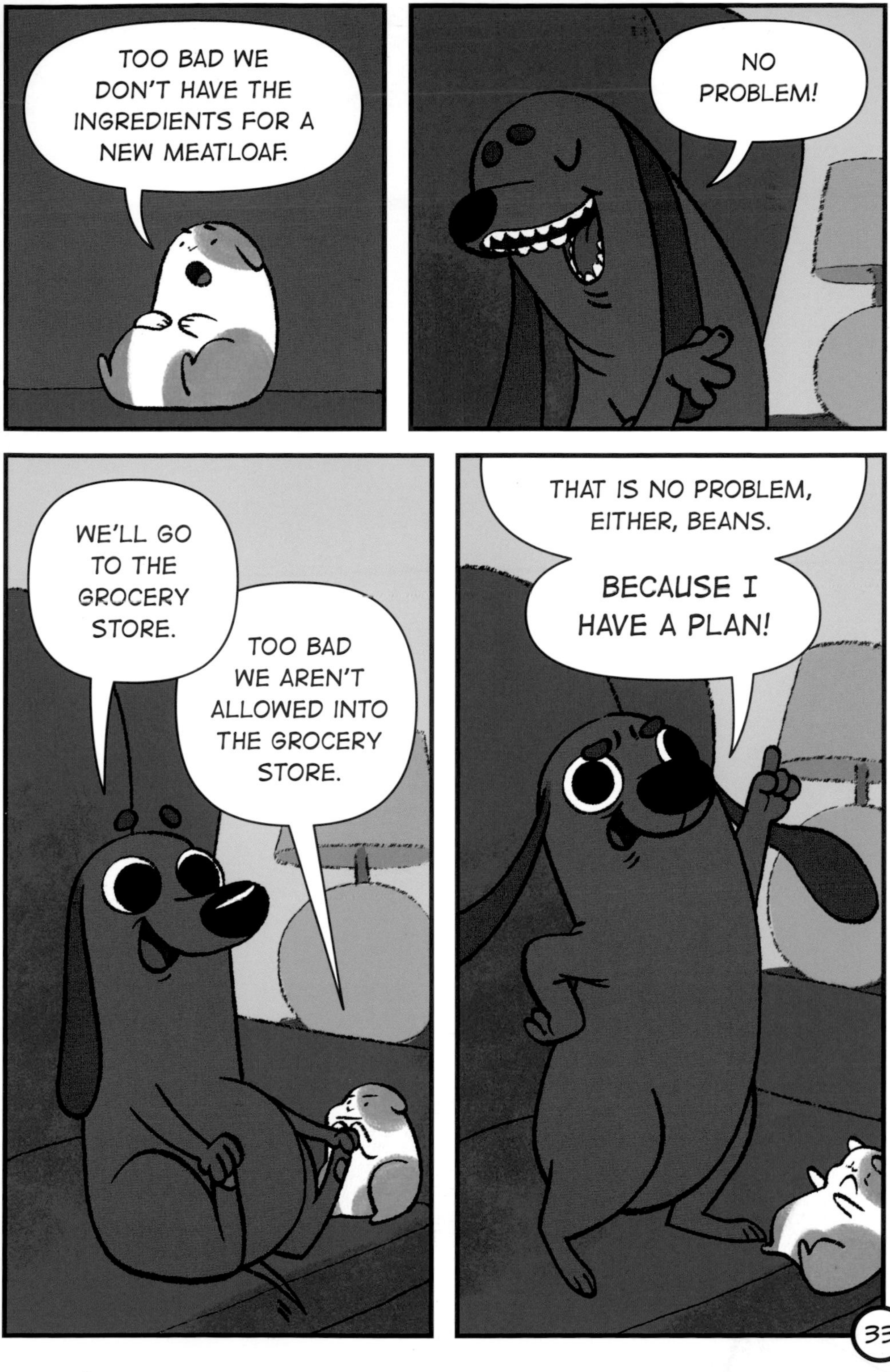
TOO BAD WE DON'T HAVE THE INGREDIENTS FOR A NEW MEATLOAF.
NO PROBLEM!
WE'LL GO TO THE GROCERY STORE.
TOO BAD WE AREN'T ALLOWED INTO THE GROCERY STORE.
THAT IS NO PROBLEM, EITHER, BEANS.
BECAUSE I HAVE A PLAN!

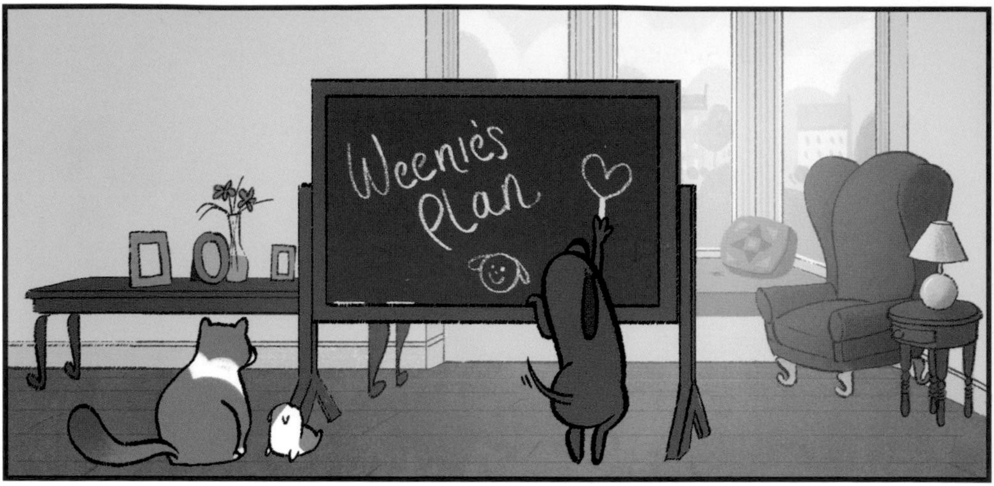
Weenie's Plan

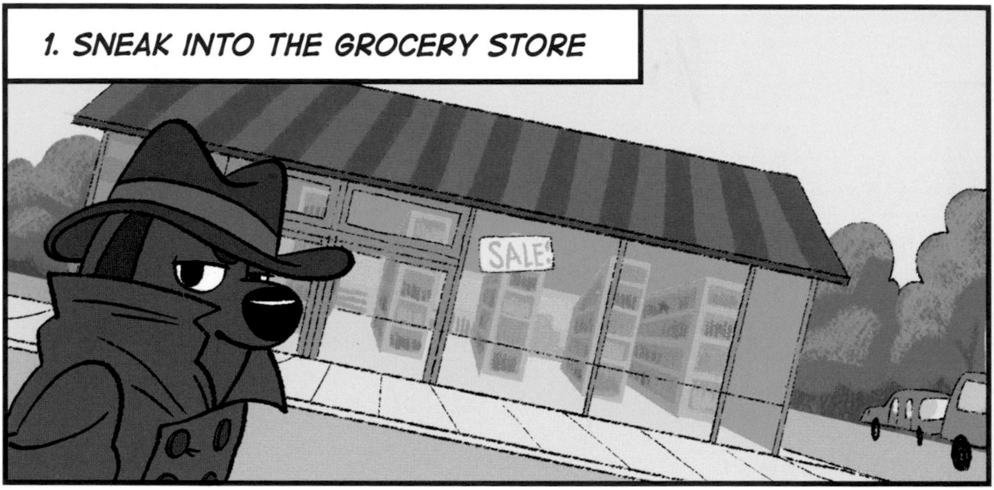
1. SNEAK INTO THE GROCERY STORE
SALE!

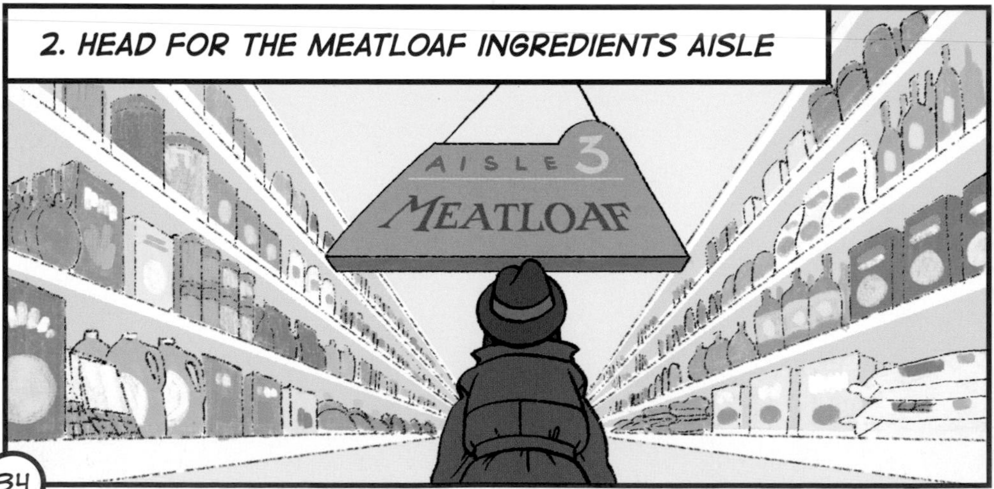
2. HEAD FOR THE MEATLOAF INGREDIENTS AISLE
AISLE 3
MEATLOAF

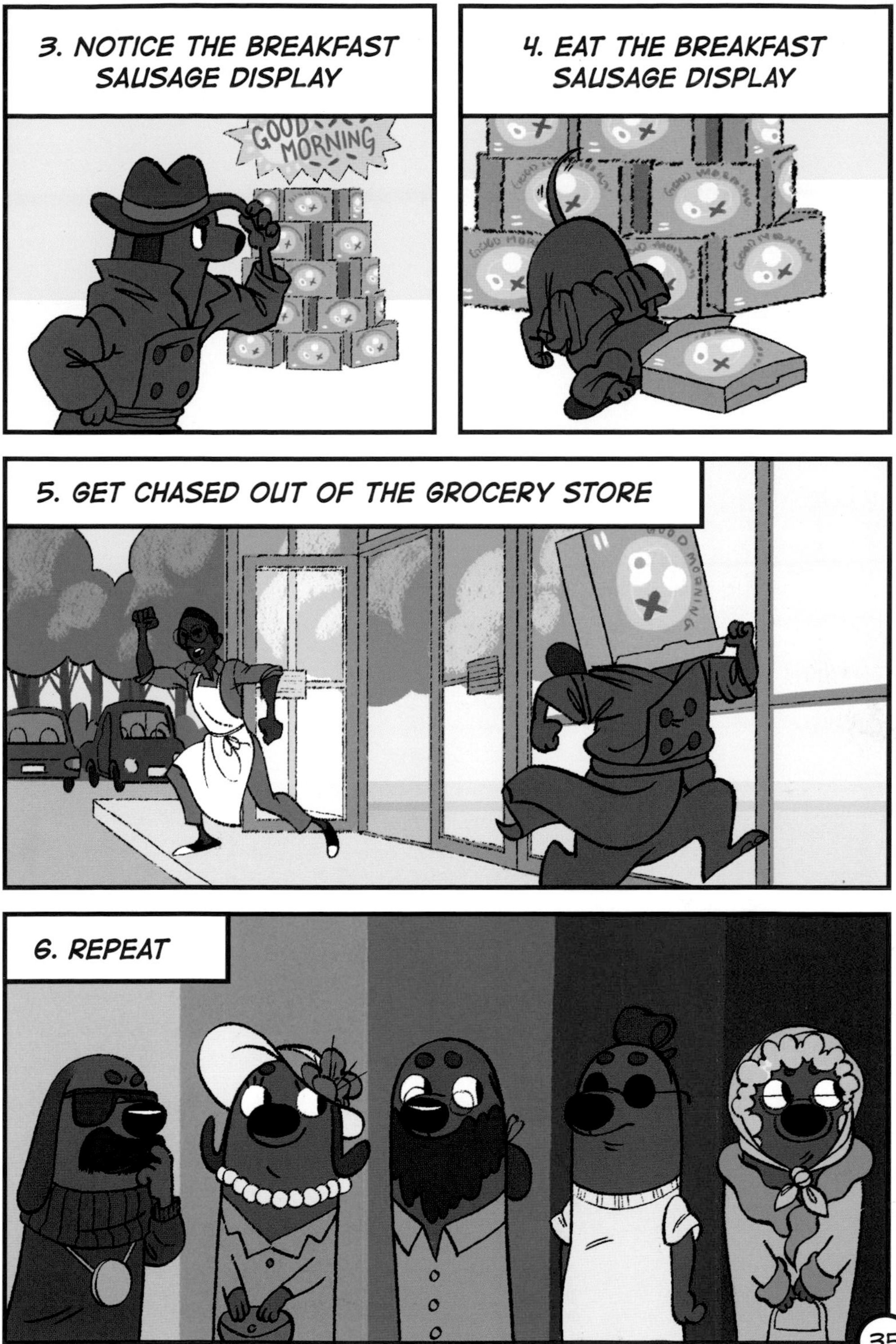
3. NOTICE THE BREAKFAST SAUSAGE DISPLAY
GOOD MORNING
4. EAT THE BREAKFAST SAUSAGE DISPLAY
5. GET CHASED OUT OF THE GROCERY STORE
GOOD MORNING
6. REPEAT

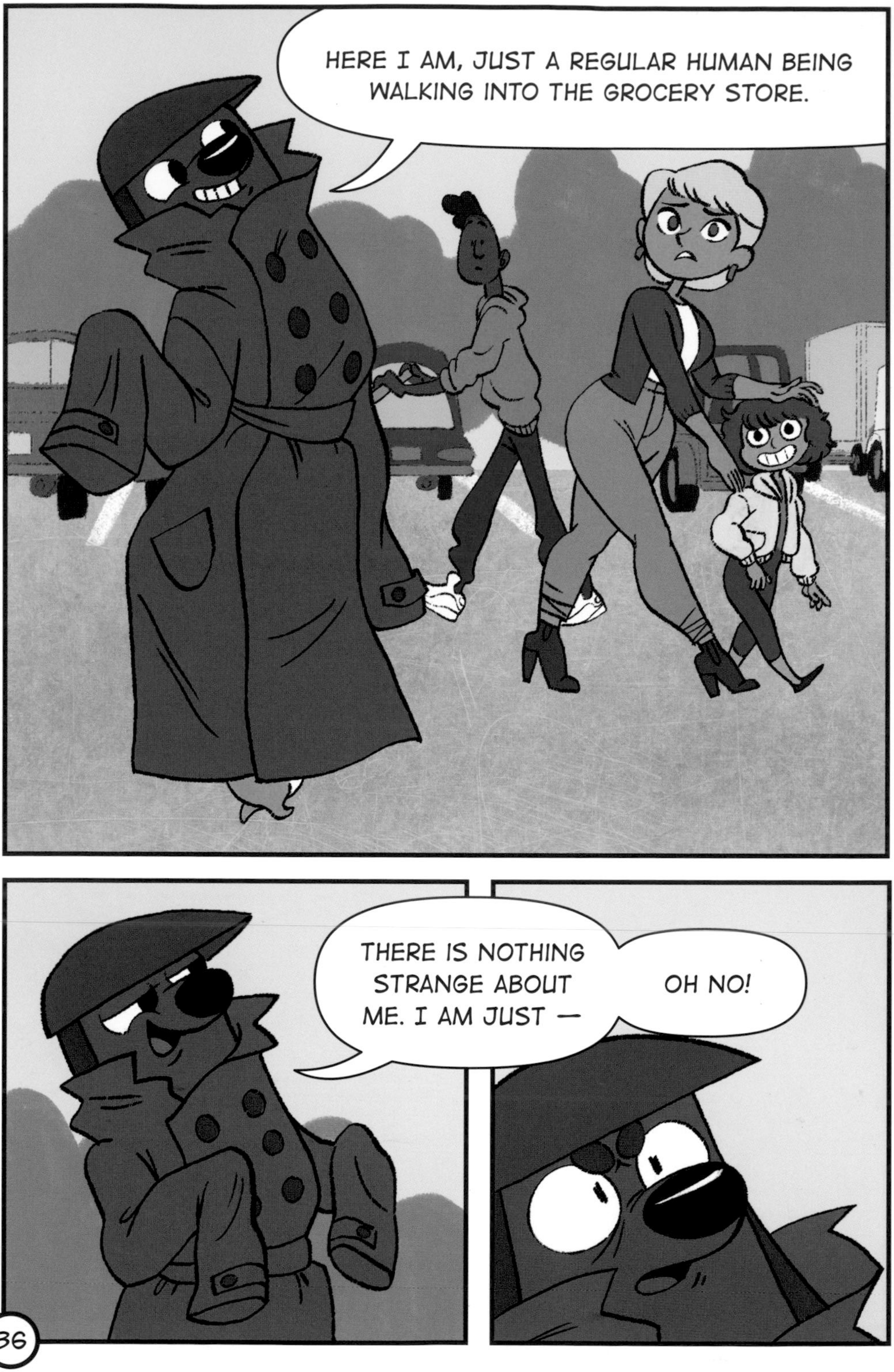
HERE I AM, JUST A REGULAR HUMAN BEING WALKING INTO THE GROCERY STORE.
THERE IS NOTHING STRANGE ABOUT ME. I AM JUST —
OH NO!

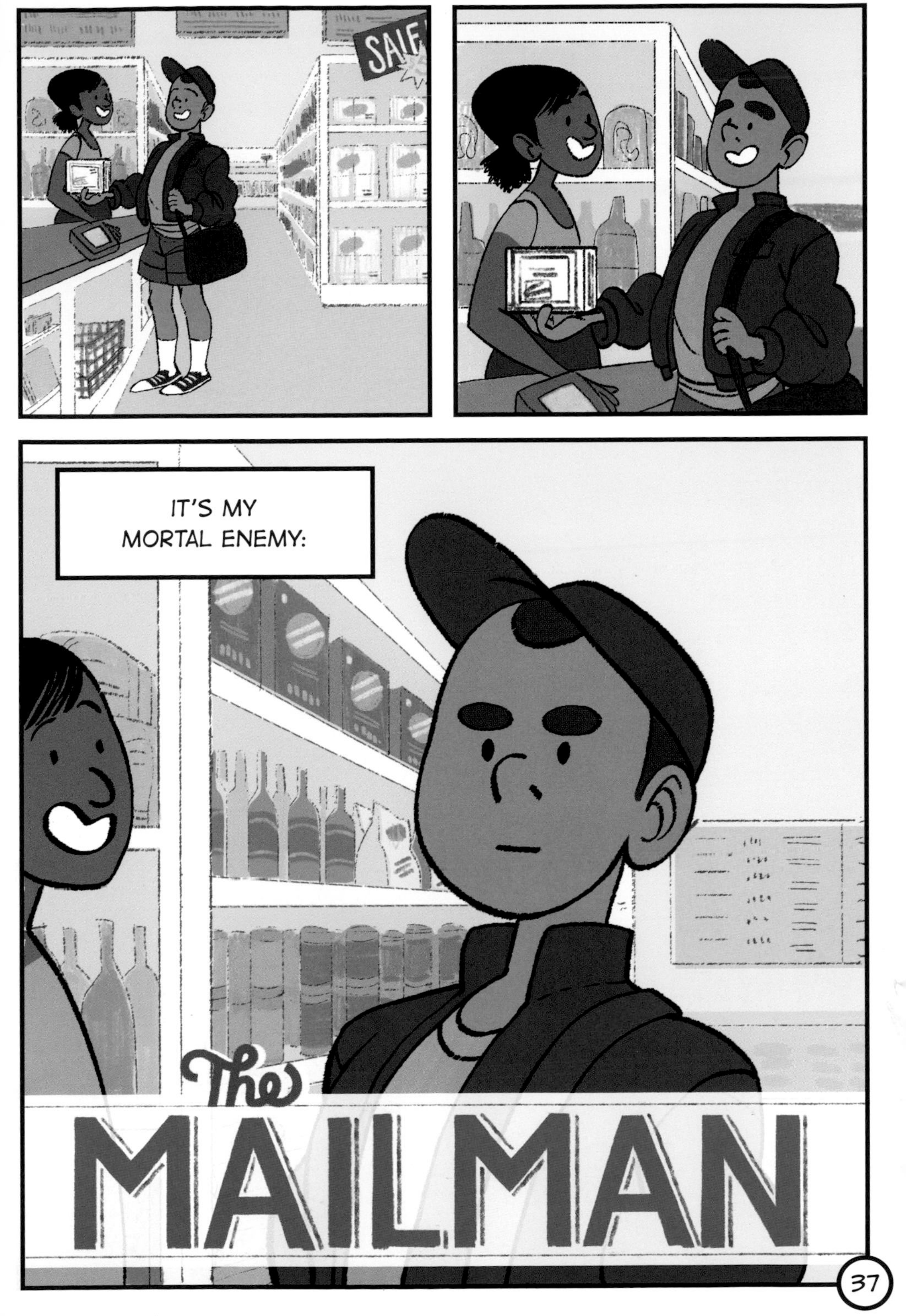
SALE
IT'S MY
MORTAL ENEMY:
The
MAILMAN

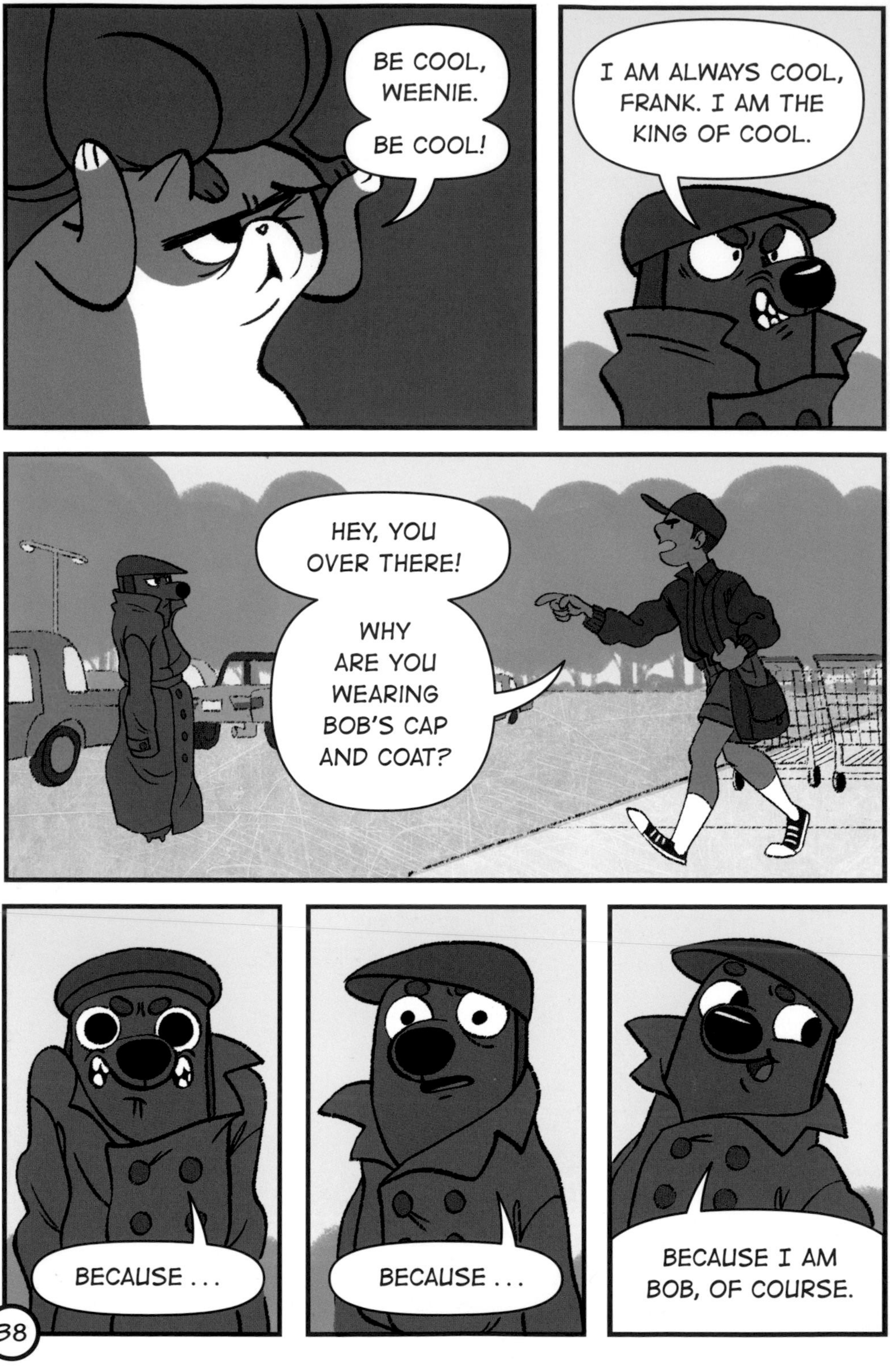
BE COOL, WEENIE.
BE COOL!
I AM ALWAYS COOL, FRANK. I AM THE KING OF COOL.
HEY, YOU OVER THERE!
WHY ARE YOU WEARING BOB'S CAP AND COAT?
BECAUSE . . .
BECAUSE . . .
BECAUSE I AM BOB, OF COURSE.

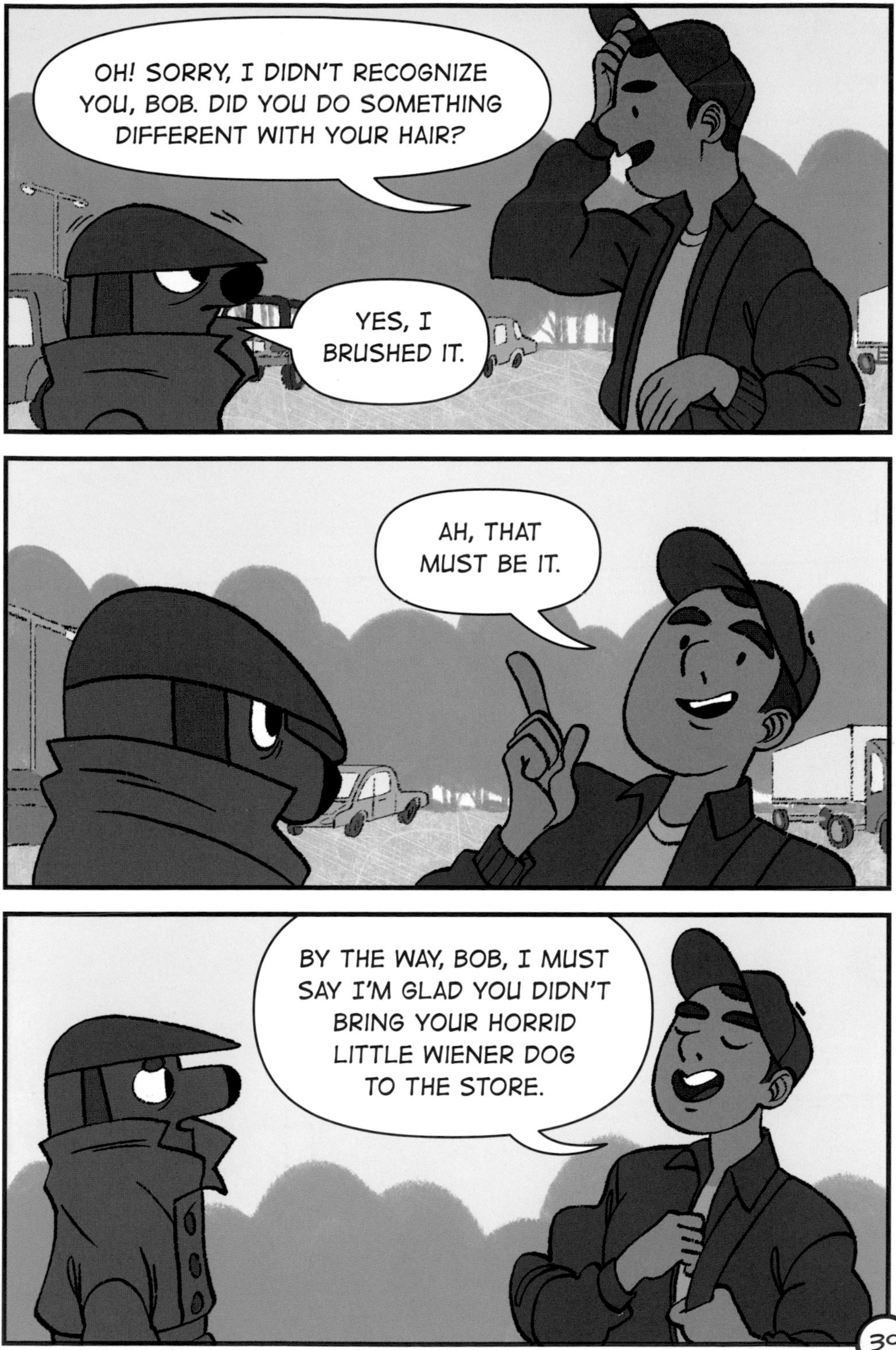
OH! SORRY, I DIDN'T RECOGNIZE YOU, BOB. DID YOU DO SOMETHING DIFFERENT WITH YOUR HAIR?
YES, I BRUSHED IT.
AH, THAT MUST BE IT.
BY THE WAY, BOB, I MUST SAY I'M GLAD YOU DIDN'T BRING YOUR HORRID LITTLE WIENER DOG TO THE STORE.

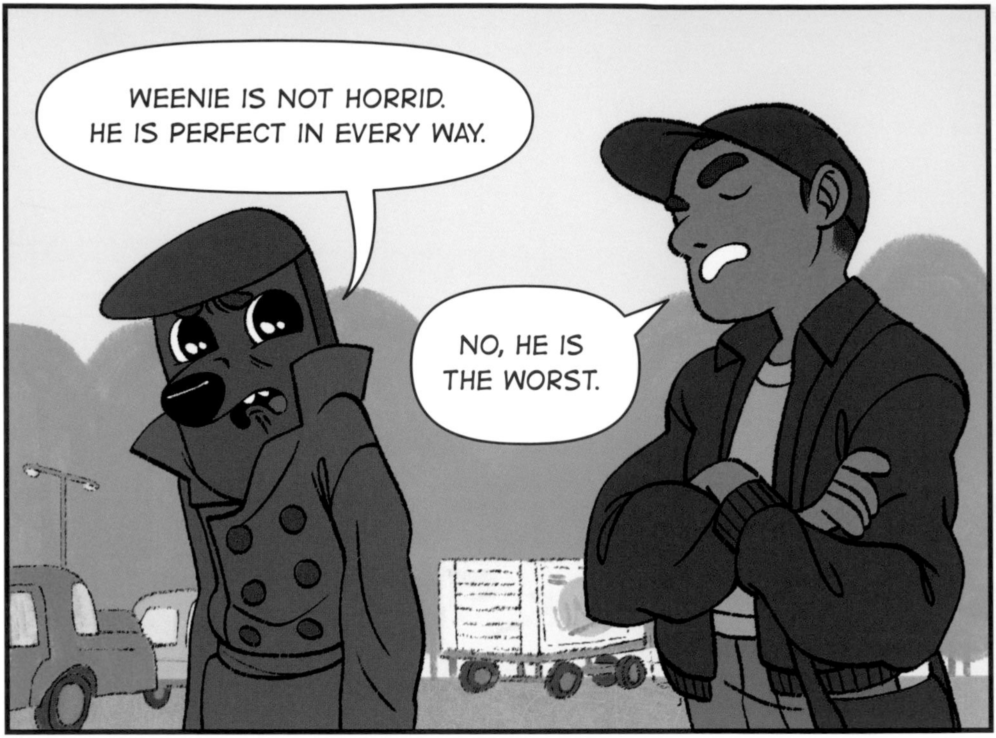
WEENIE IS NOT HORRID.
HE IS PERFECT IN EVERY WAY.
NO, HE IS THE WORST.

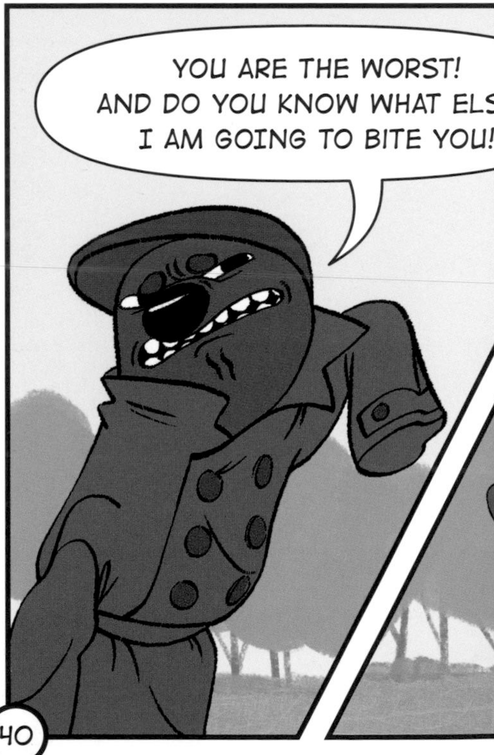
YOU ARE THE WORST!
AND DO YOU KNOW WHAT ELSE?
I AM GOING TO BITE YOU!

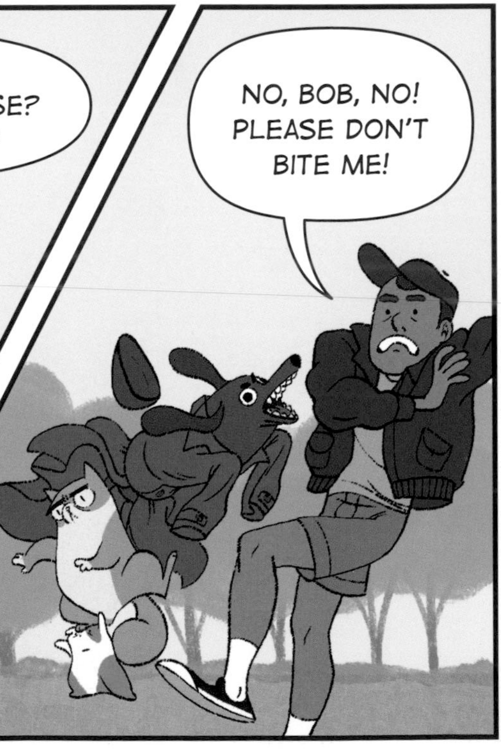
NO, BOB, NO!
PLEASE DON'T
BITE ME!

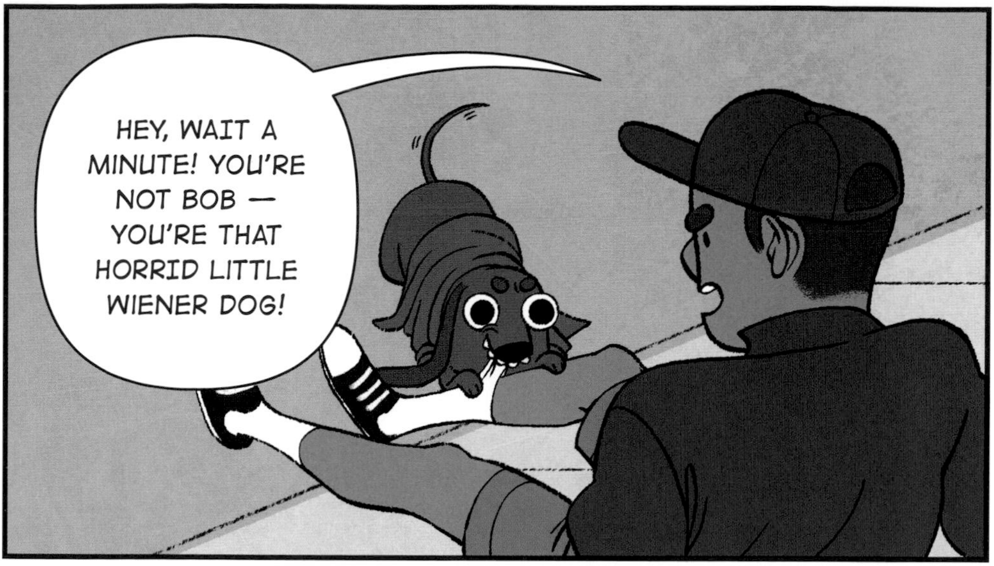
HEY, WAIT A MINUTE! YOU'RE NOT BOB — YOU'RE THAT HORRID LITTLE WIENER DOG!

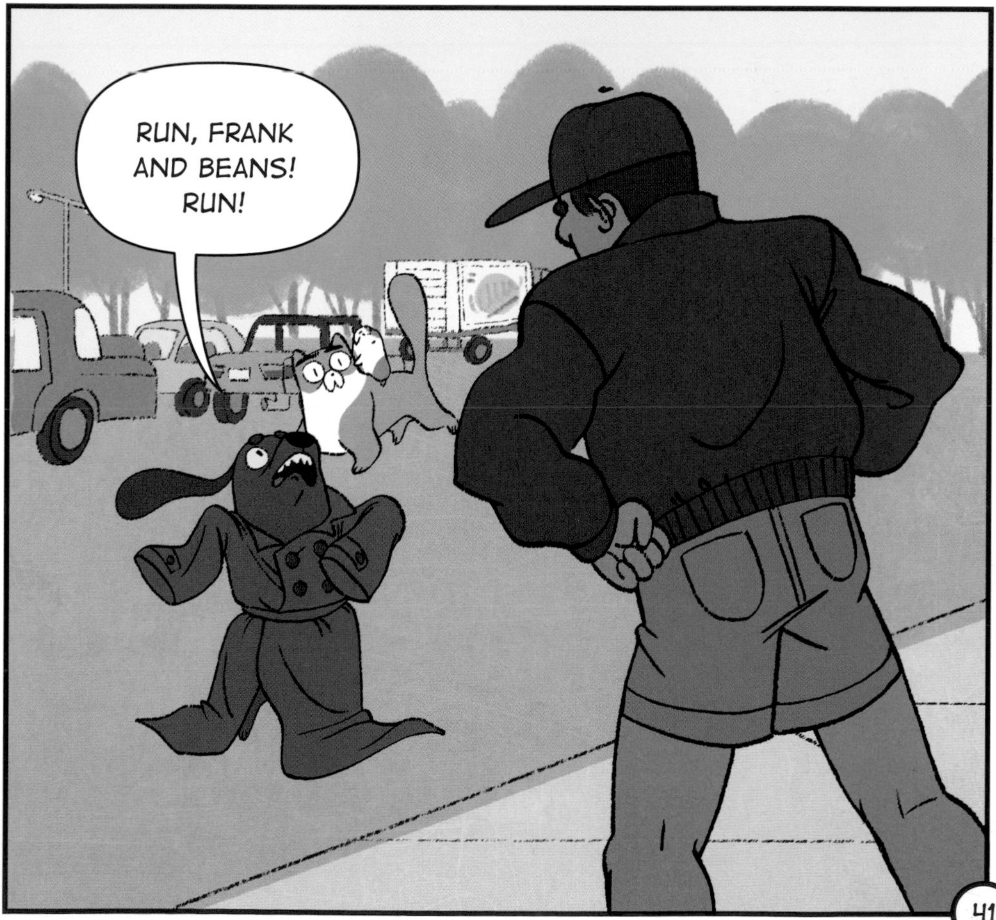
RUN, FRANK AND BEANS! RUN!

Chapter 5
Wild Meatloaf Surprise

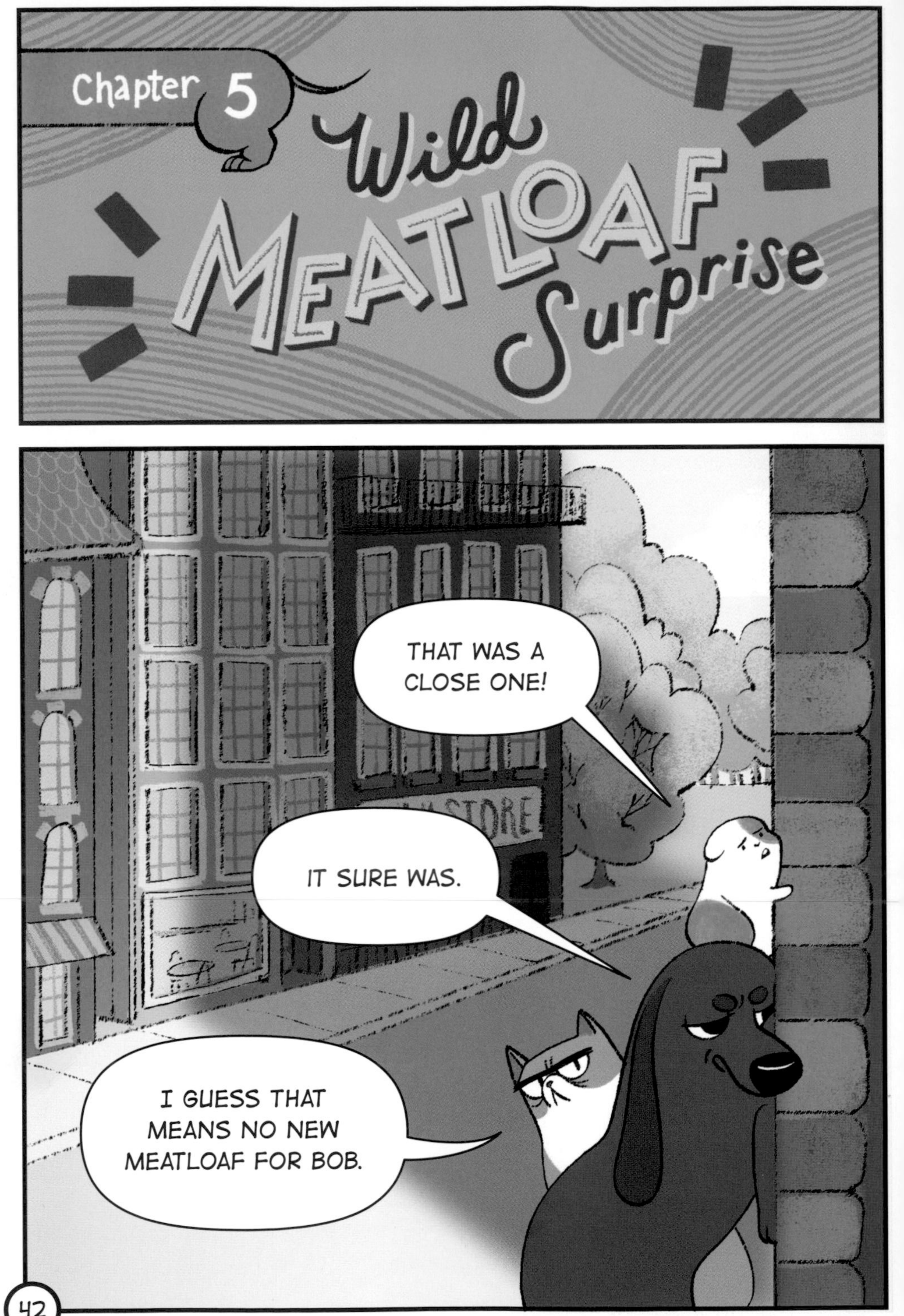
THAT WAS A CLOSE ONE!
IT SURE WAS.
I GUESS THAT MEANS NO NEW MEATLOAF FOR BOB.

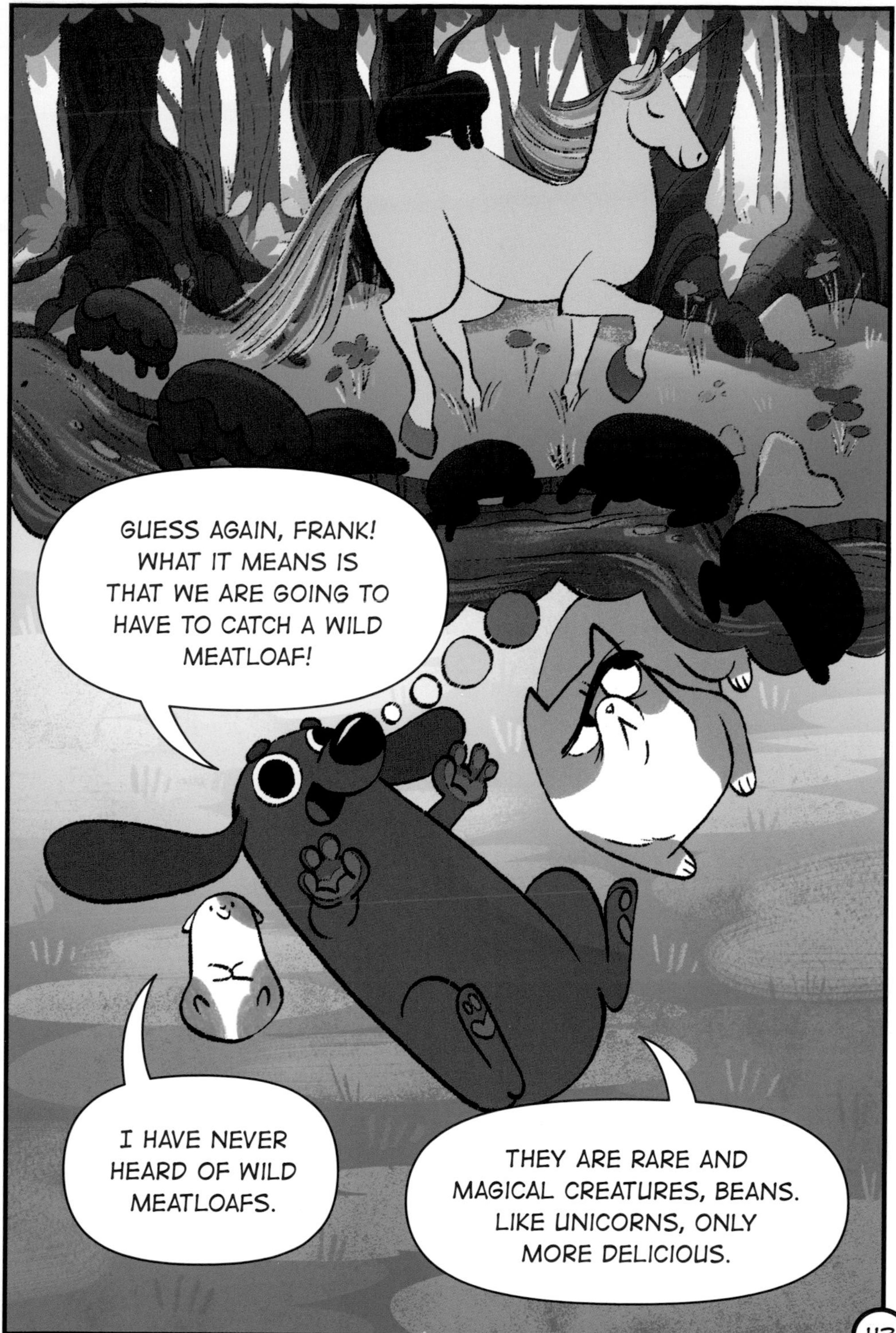
GUESS AGAIN, FRANK! WHAT IT MEANS IS THAT WE ARE GOING TO HAVE TO CATCH A WILD MEATLOAF!
I HAVE NEVER HEARD OF WILD MEATLOAFS.
THEY ARE RARE AND MAGICAL CREATURES, BEANS. LIKE UNICORNS, ONLY MORE DELICIOUS.

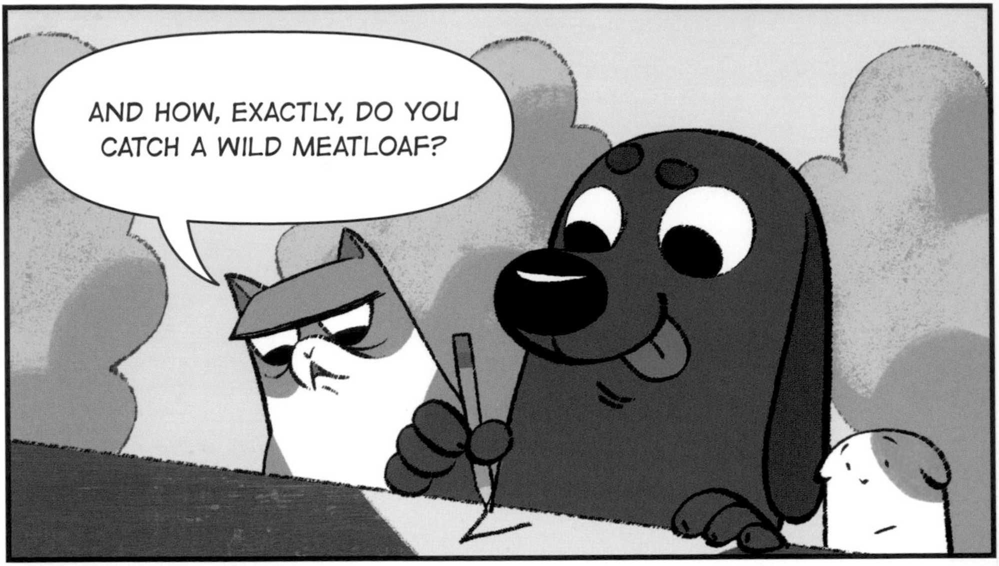
AND HOW, EXACTLY, DO YOU CATCH A WILD MEATLOAF?

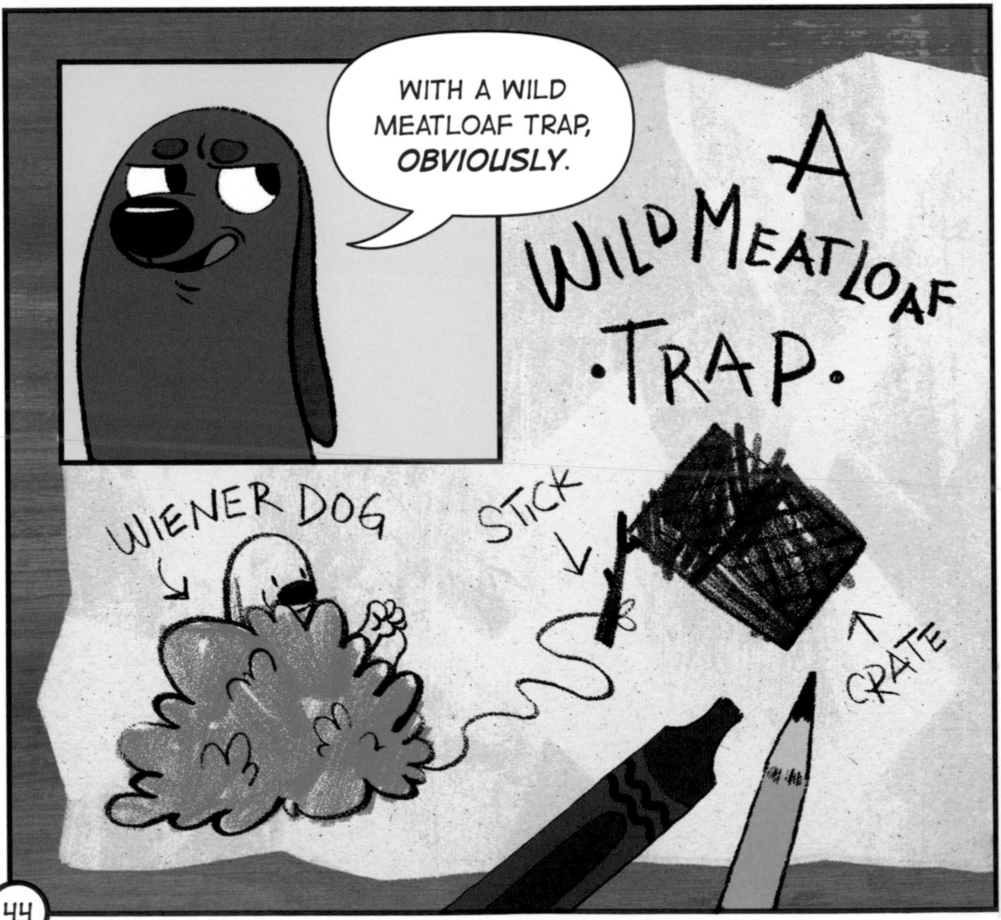
WITH A WILD MEATLOAF TRAP, *OBVIOUSLY*.
A WILD MEATLOAF TRAP
WIENER DOG
STICK
CRATE

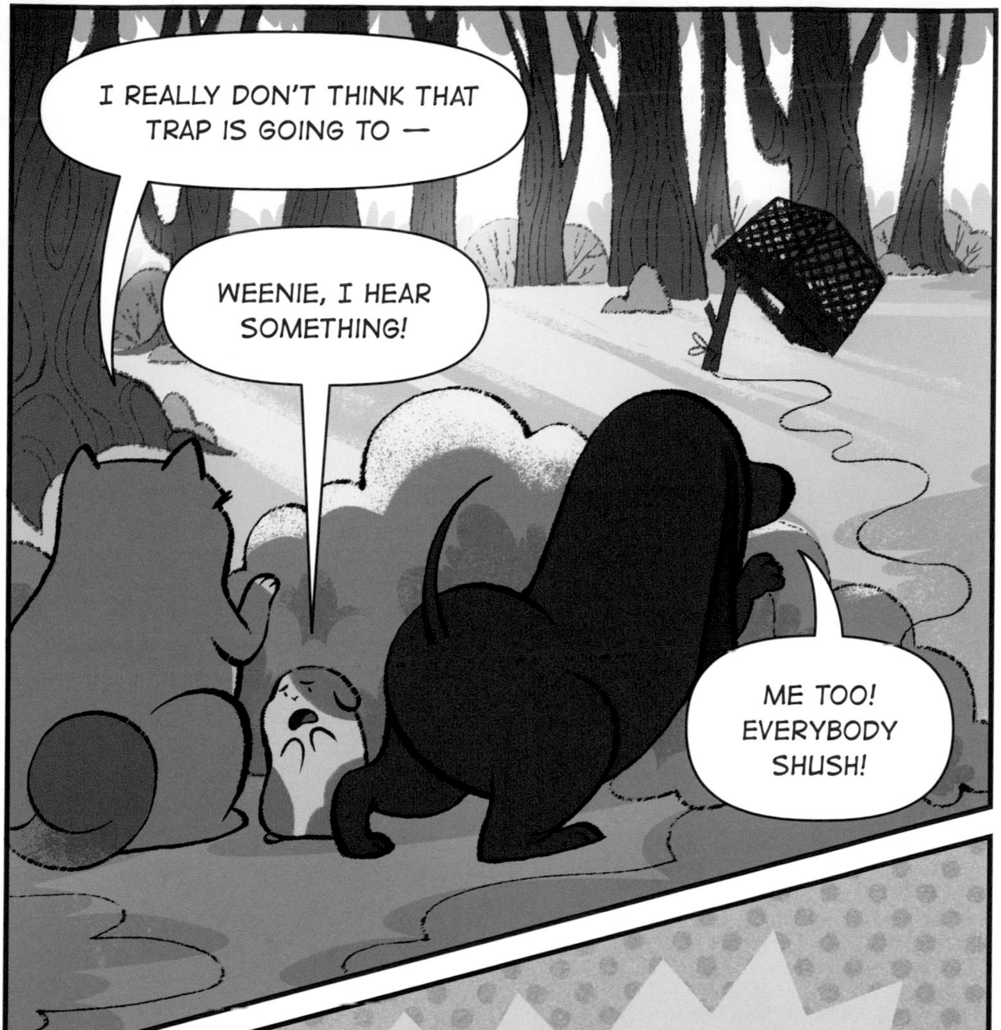
I REALLY DON'T THINK THAT TRAP IS GOING TO —
WEENIE, I HEAR SOMETHING!
ME TOO! EVERYBODY SHUSH!

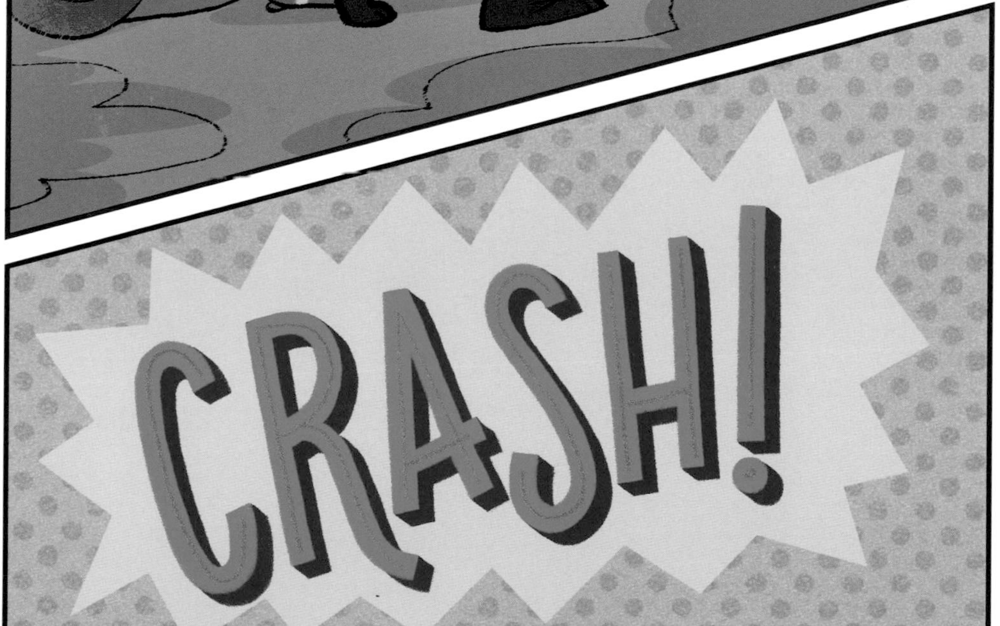
CRASH!

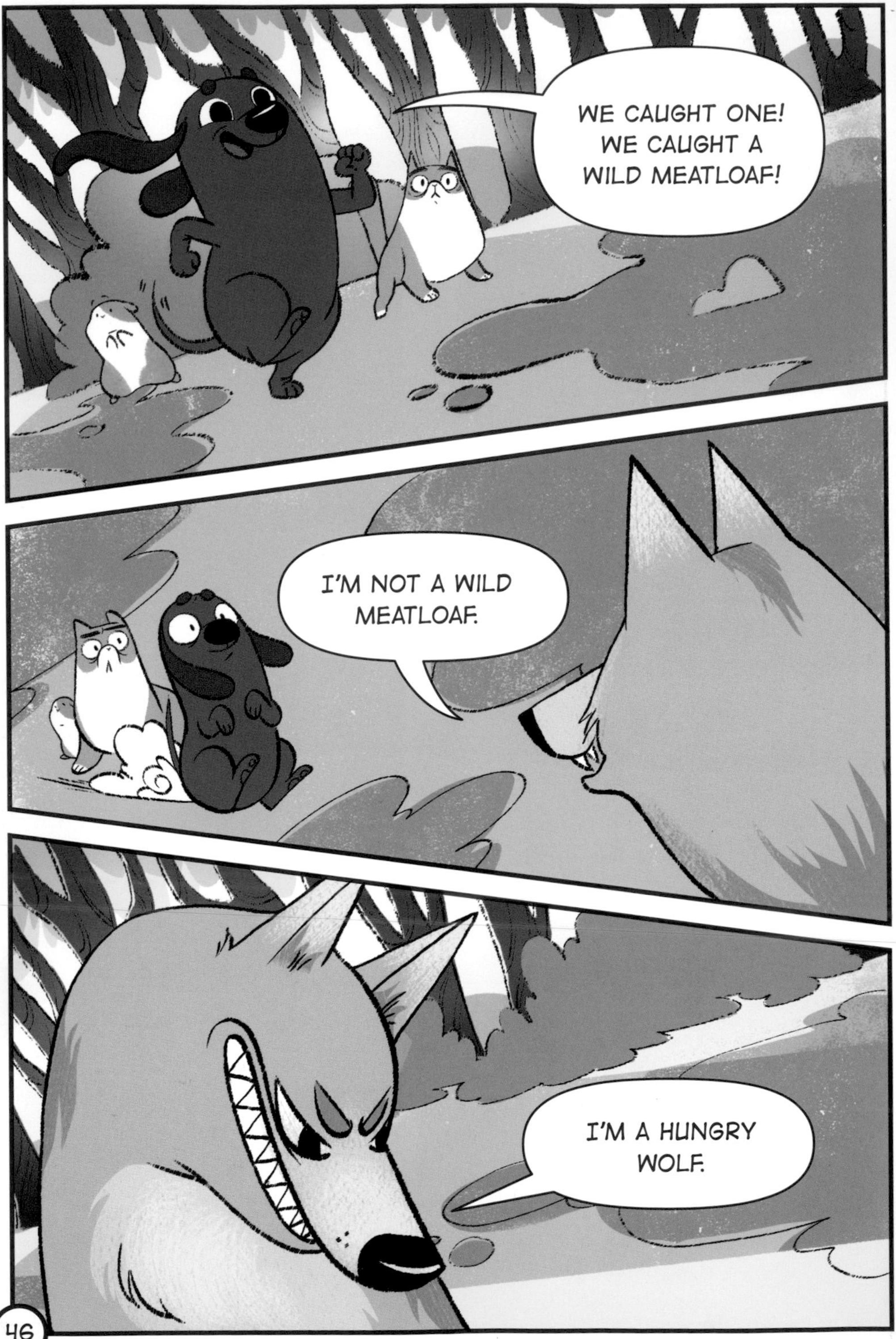
WE CAUGHT ONE! WE CAUGHT A WILD MEATLOAF!
I'M NOT A WILD MEATLOAF.
I'M A HUNGRY WOLF.

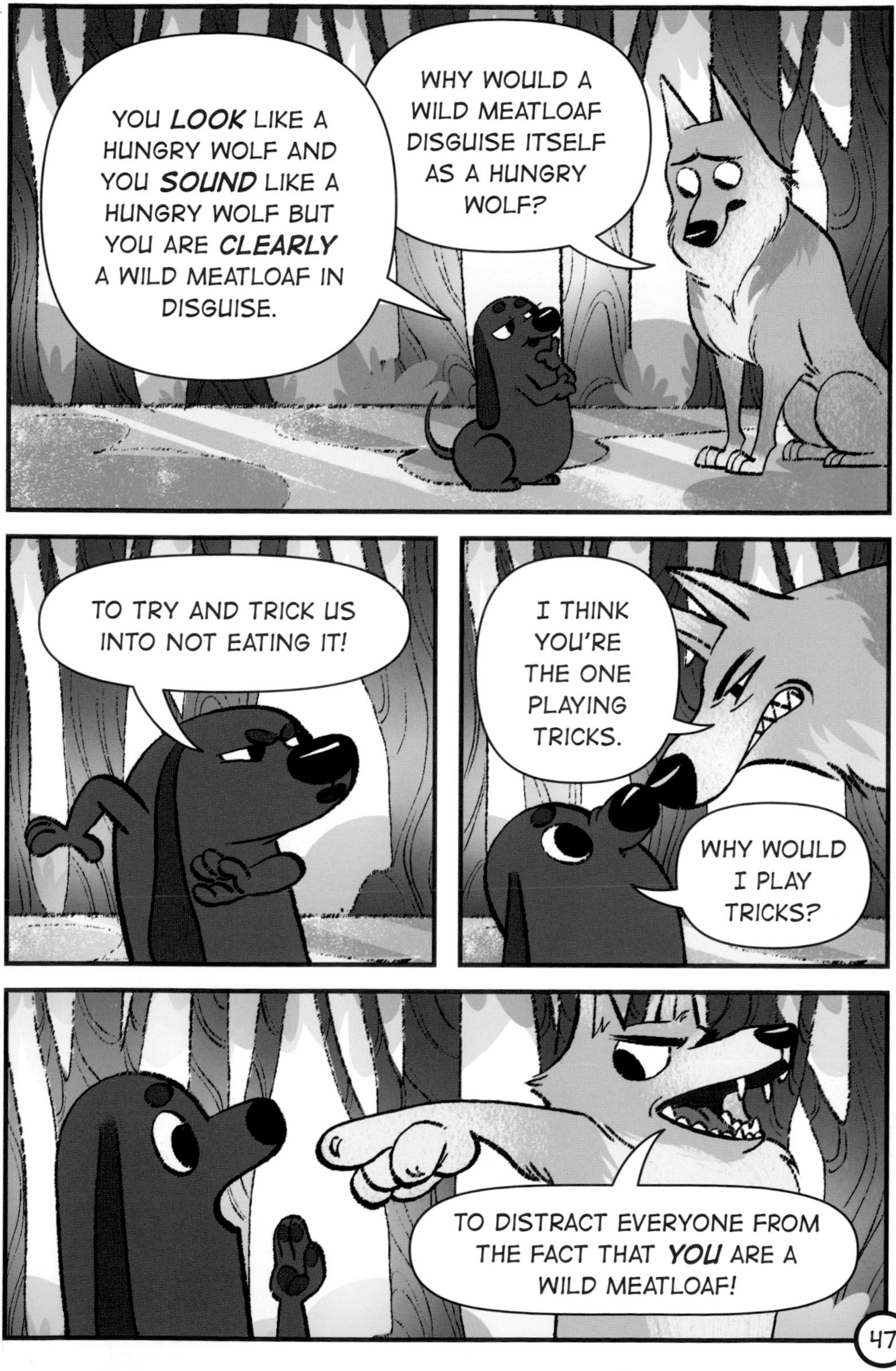
YOU LOOK LIKE A HUNGRY WOLF AND YOU SOUND LIKE A HUNGRY WOLF BUT YOU ARE CLEARLY A WILD MEATLOAF IN DISGUISE.
WHY WOULD A WILD MEATLOAF DISGUISE ITSELF AS A HUNGRY WOLF?
TO TRY AND TRICK US INTO NOT EATING IT!
I THINK YOU'RE THE ONE PLAYING TRICKS.
WHY WOULD I PLAY TRICKS?
TO DISTRACT EVERYONE FROM THE FACT THAT YOU ARE A WILD MEATLOAF!

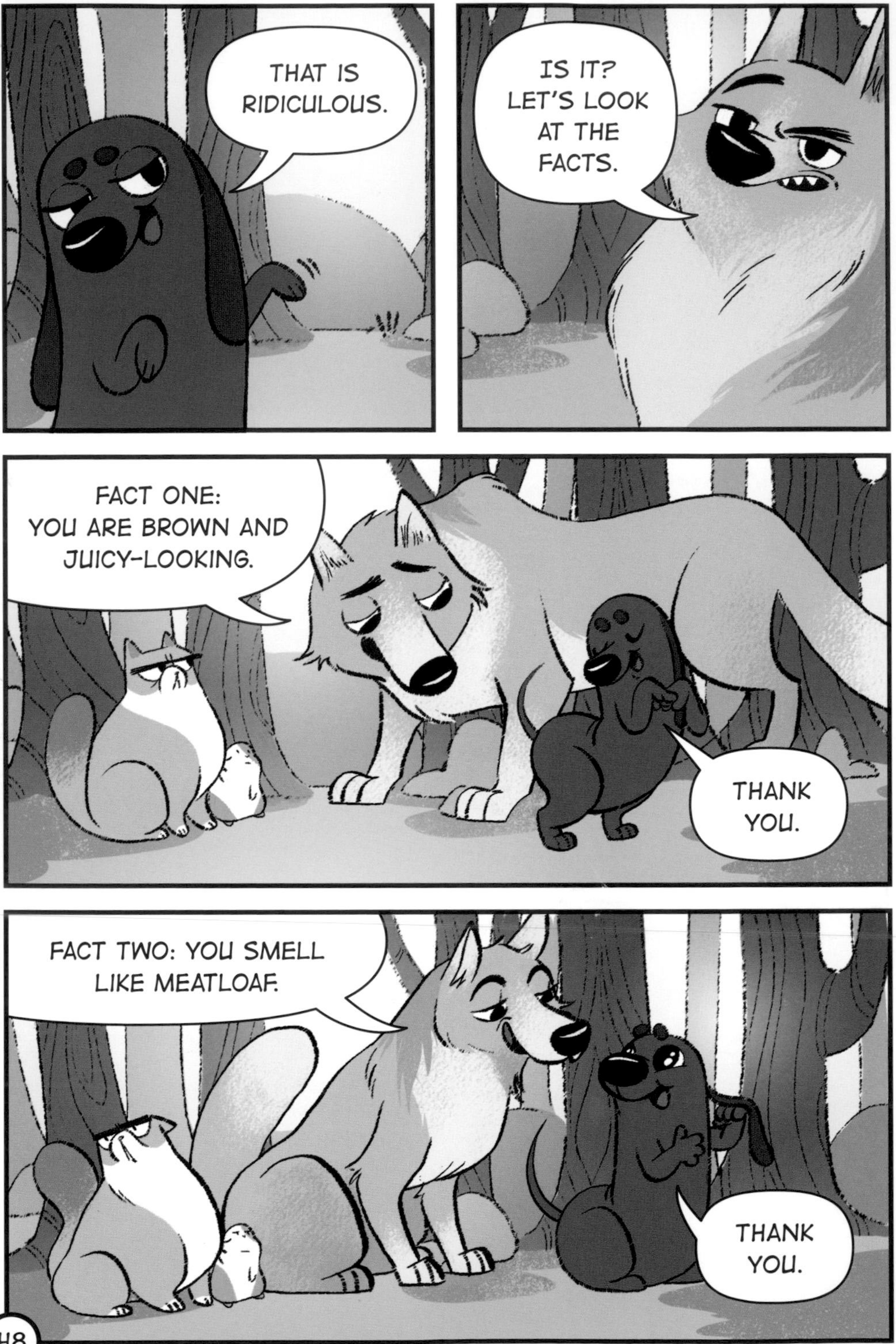
THAT IS RIDICULOUS.
IS IT? LET'S LOOK AT THE FACTS.
FACT ONE: YOU ARE BROWN AND JUICY-LOOKING.
THANK YOU.
FACT TWO: YOU SMELL LIKE MEATLOAF.
THANK YOU.

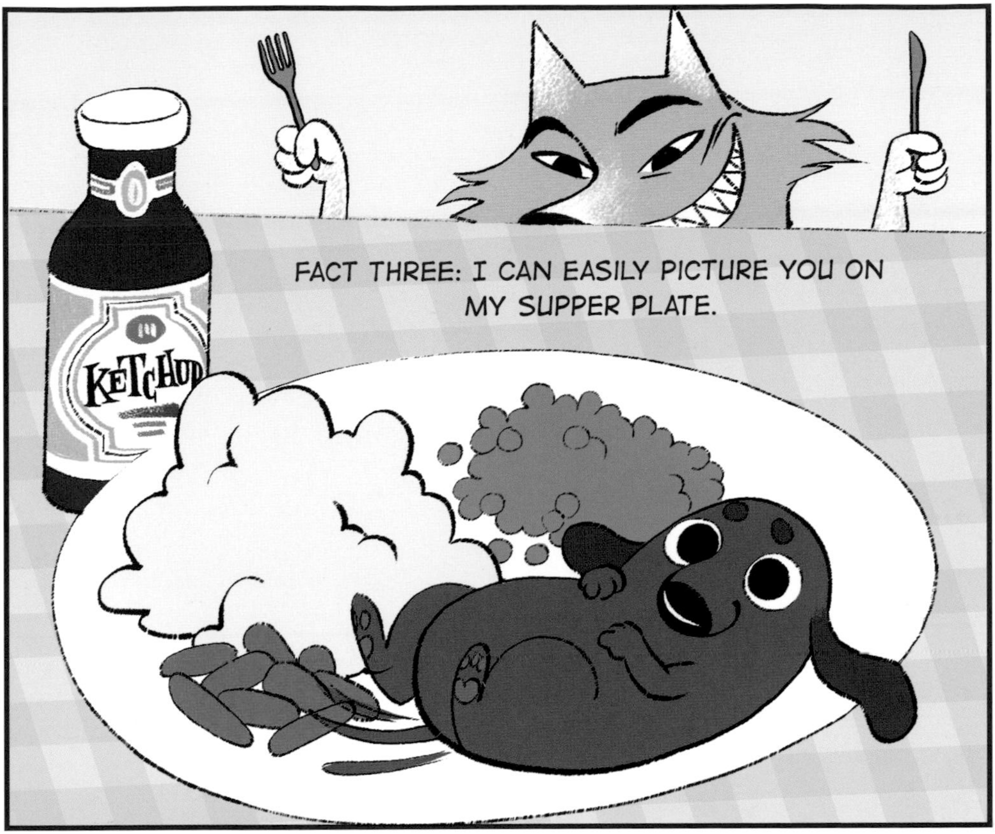
KETCHUP
FACT THREE: I CAN EASILY PICTURE YOU ON MY SUPPER PLATE.

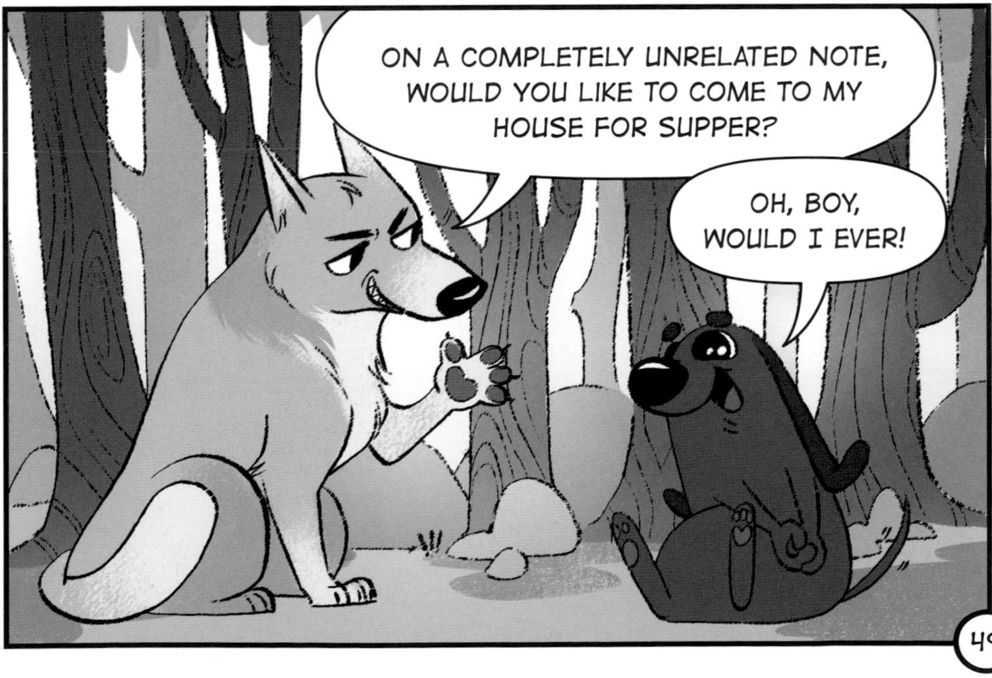
ON A COMPLETELY UNRELATED NOTE, WOULD YOU LIKE TO COME TO MY HOUSE FOR SUPPER?
OH, BOY, WOULD I EVER!

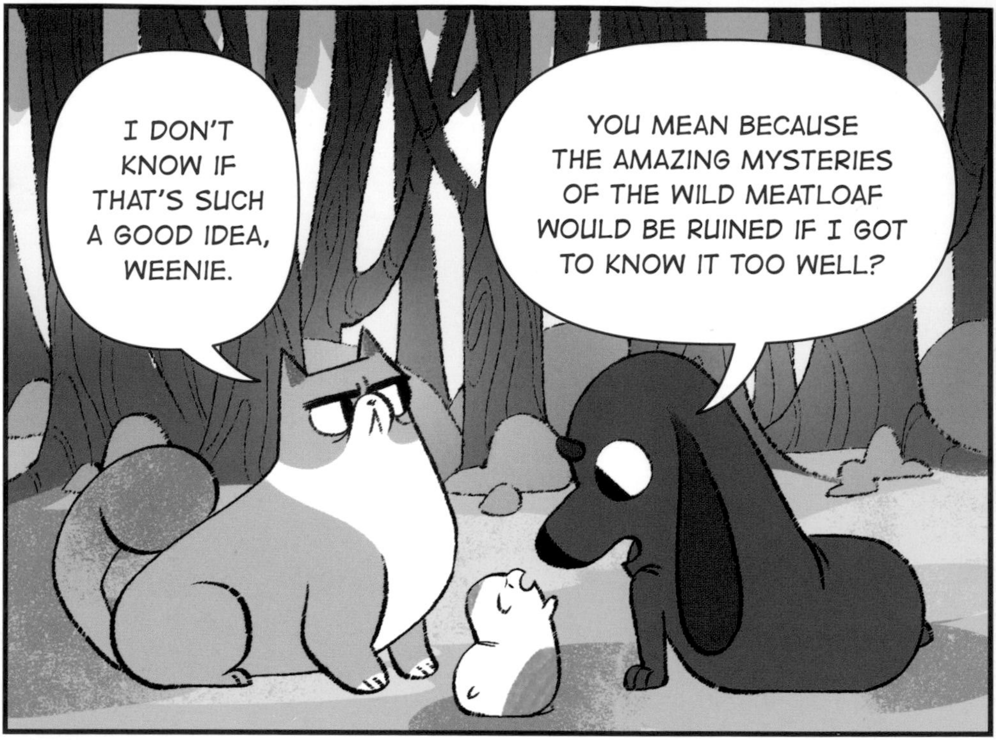
I DON'T KNOW IF THAT'S SUCH A GOOD IDEA, WEENIE.
YOU MEAN BECAUSE THE AMAZING MYSTERIES OF THE WILD MEATLOAF WOULD BE RUINED IF I GOT TO KNOW IT TOO WELL?

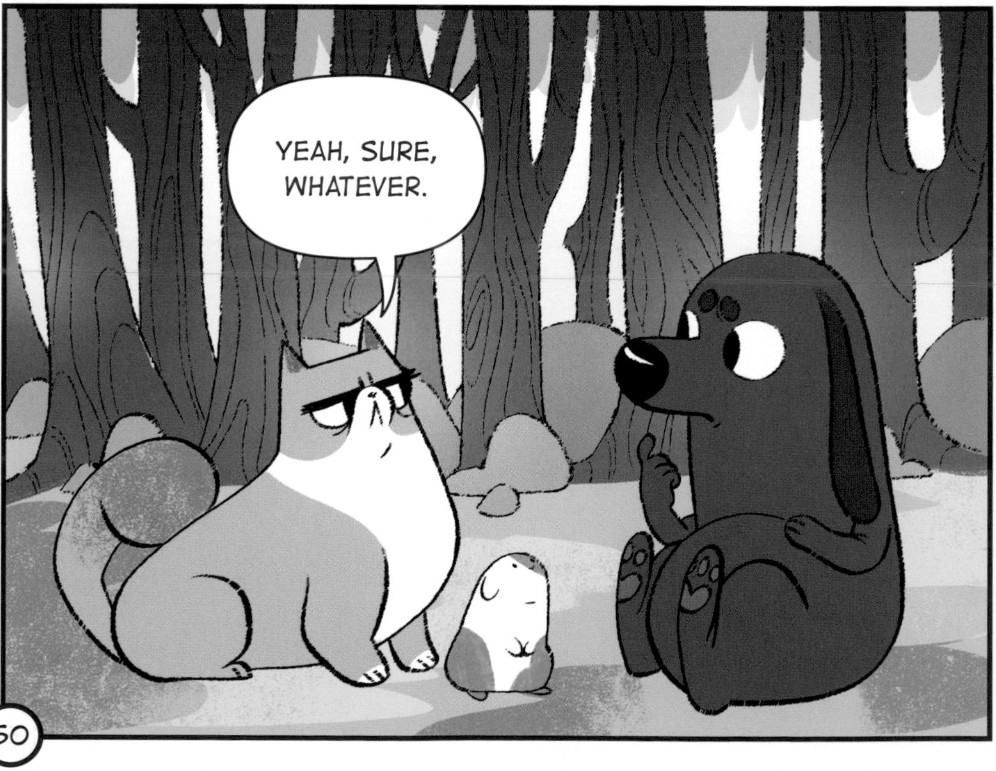
YEAH, SURE, WHATEVER.

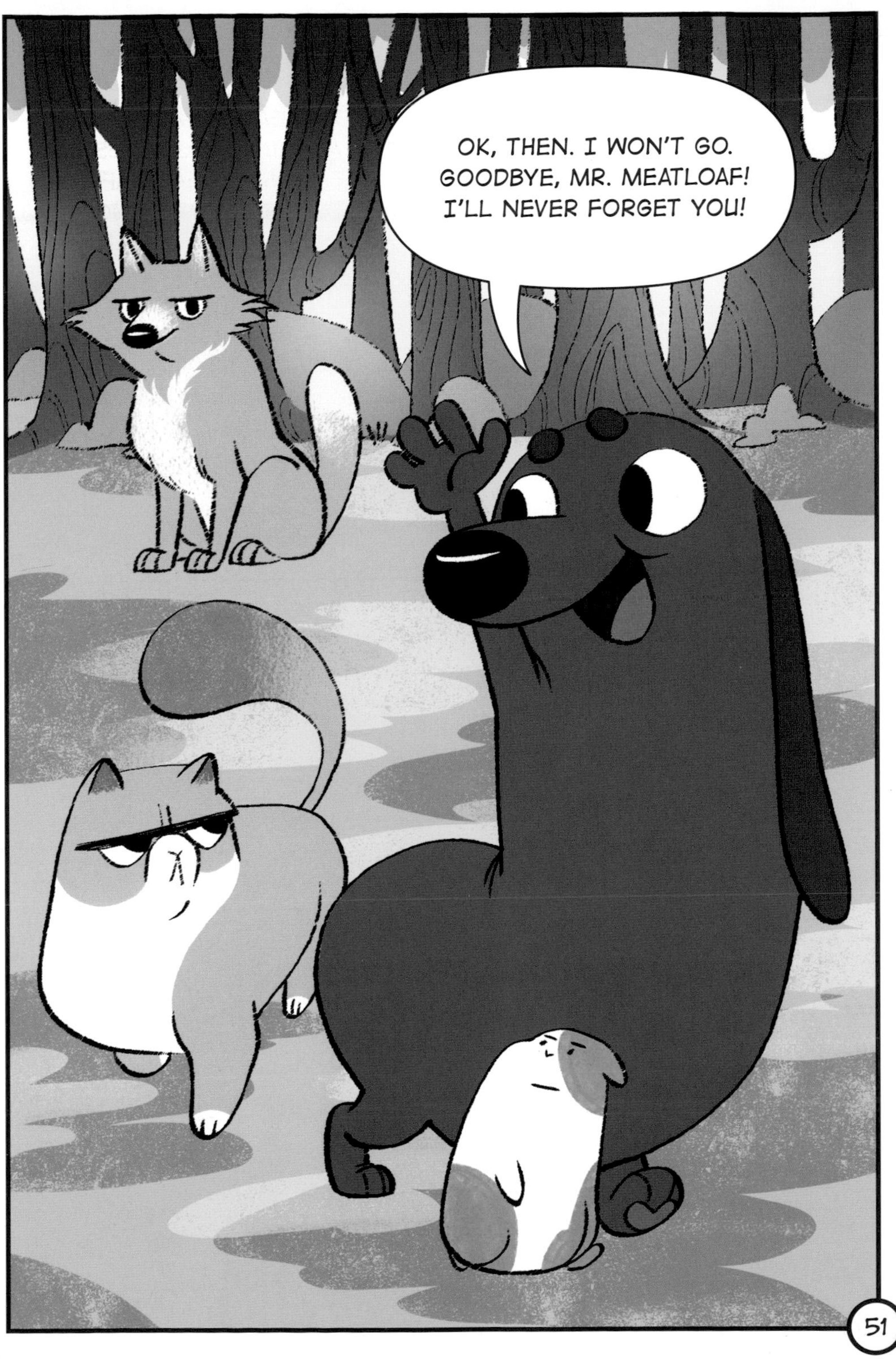
OK, THEN. I WON'T GO. GOODBYE, MR. MEATLOAF! I'LL NEVER FORGET YOU!

Chapter 6
Something Better Than MEATLOAF

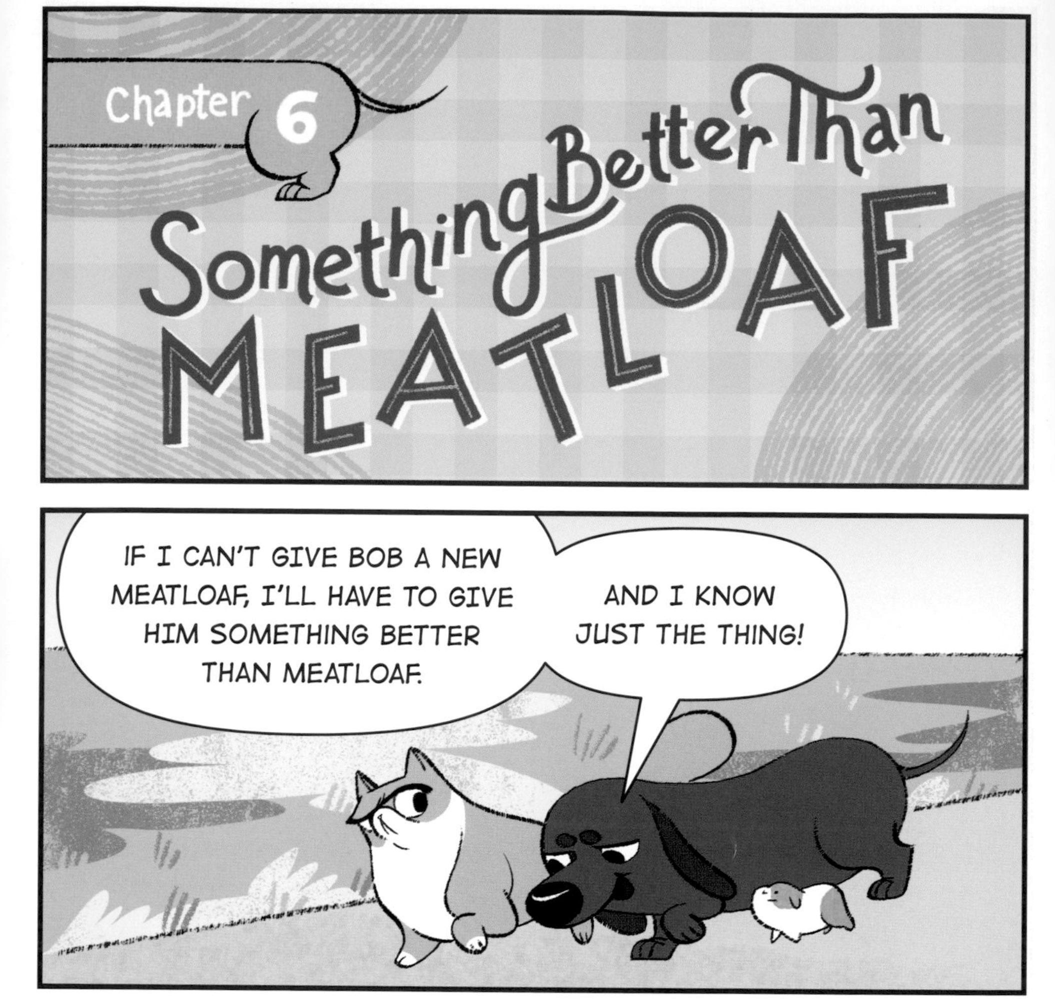
IF I CAN'T GIVE BOB A NEW MEATLOAF, I'LL HAVE TO GIVE HIM SOMETHING BETTER THAN MEATLOAF.
AND I KNOW JUST THE THING!

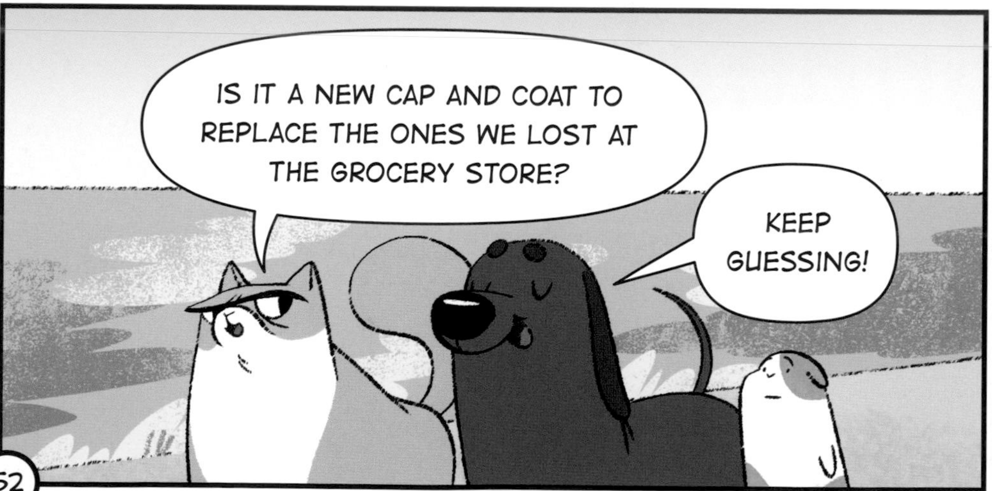
IS IT A NEW CAP AND COAT TO REPLACE THE ONES WE LOST AT THE GROCERY STORE?
KEEP GUESSING!

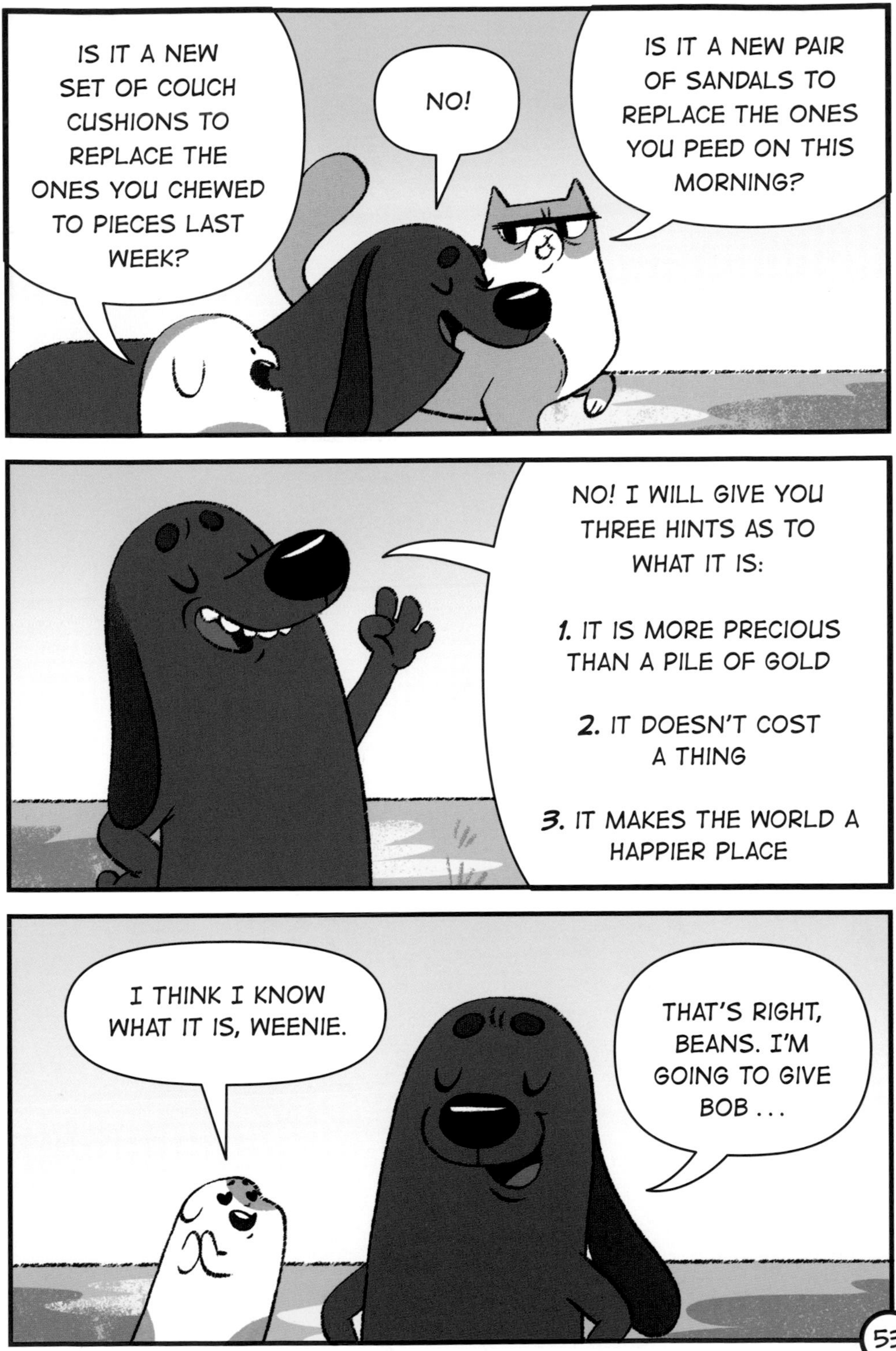
IS IT A NEW SET OF COUCH CUSHIONS TO REPLACE THE ONES YOU CHEWED TO PIECES LAST WEEK?
NO!
IS IT A NEW PAIR OF SANDALS TO REPLACE THE ONES YOU PEED ON THIS MORNING?
NO! I WILL GIVE YOU THREE HINTS AS TO WHAT IT IS:
1. IT IS MORE PRECIOUS THAN A PILE OF GOLD
2. IT DOESN'T COST A THING
3. IT MAKES THE WORLD A HAPPIER PLACE
I THINK I KNOW WHAT IT IS, WEENIE.
THAT'S RIGHT, BEANS. I'M GOING TO GIVE BOB . . .

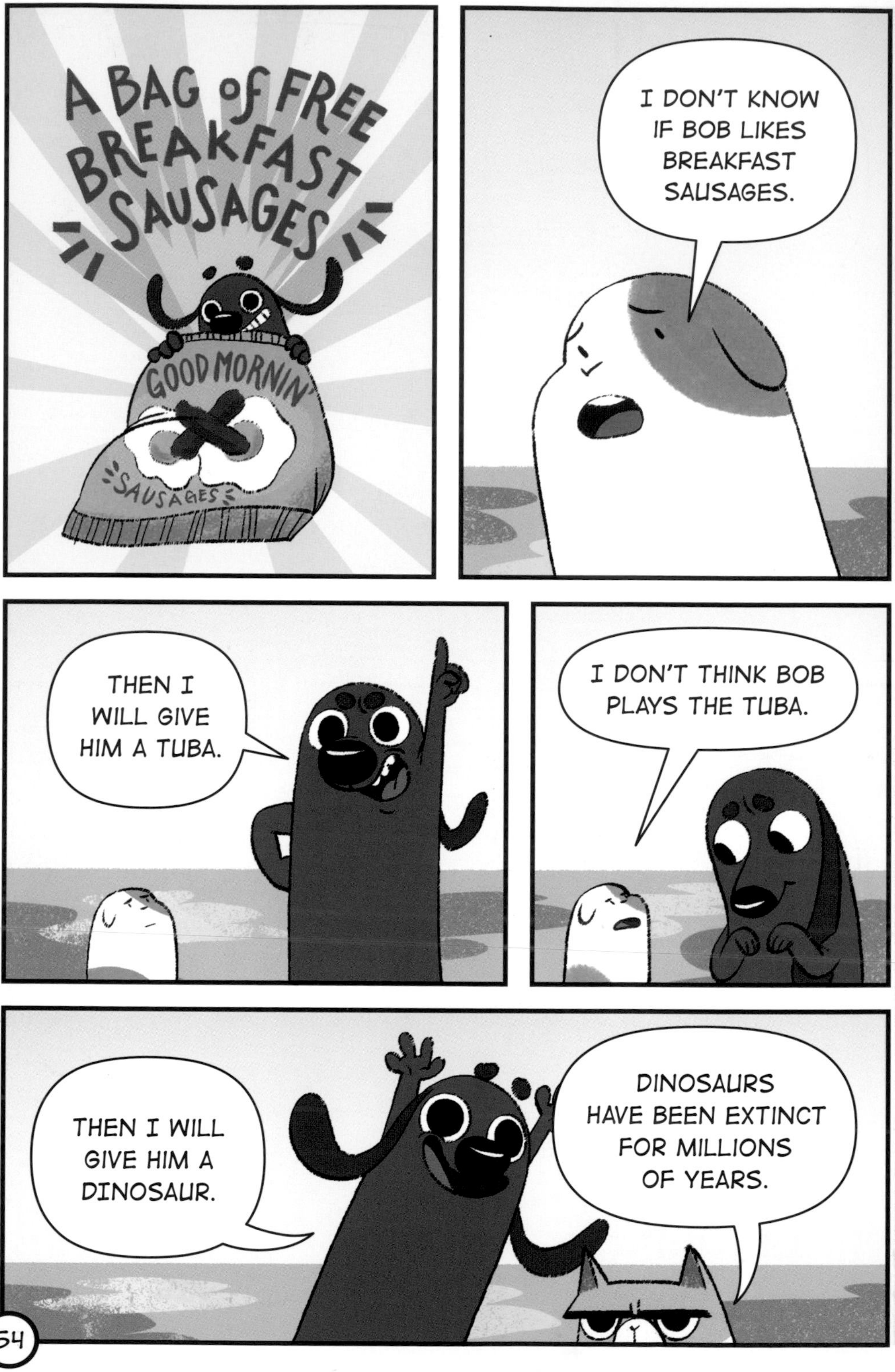
A BAG OF FREE BREAKFAST SAUSAGES
GOOD MORNIN'
SAUSAGES
I DON'T KNOW IF BOB LIKES BREAKFAST SAUSAGES.
THEN I WILL GIVE HIM A TUBA.
I DON'T THINK BOB PLAYS THE TUBA.
THEN I WILL GIVE HIM A DINOSAUR.
DINOSAURS HAVE BEEN EXTINCT FOR MILLIONS OF YEARS.

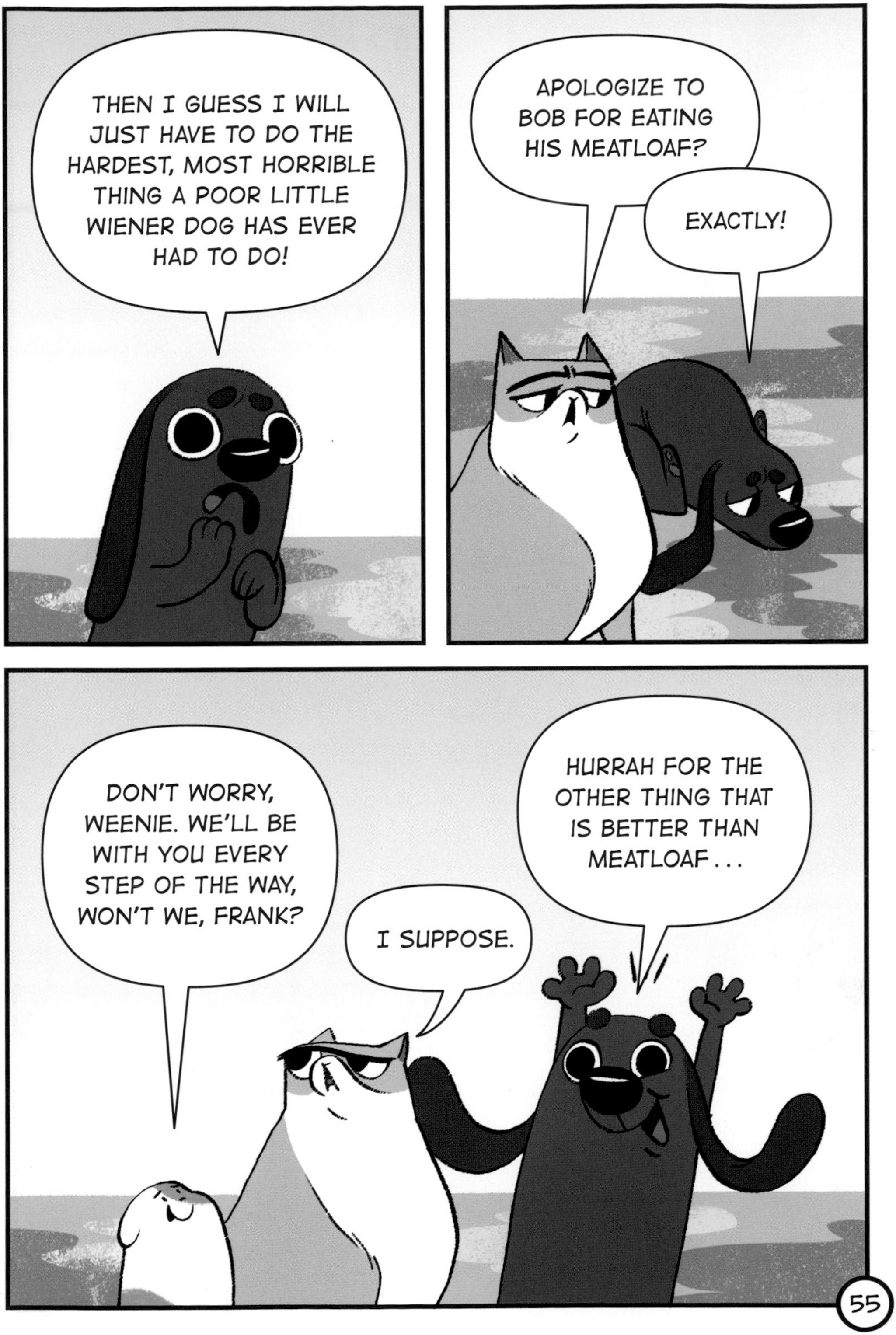
THEN I GUESS I WILL JUST HAVE TO DO THE HARDEST, MOST HORRIBLE THING A POOR LITTLE WIENER DOG HAS EVER HAD TO DO!
APOLOGIZE TO BOB FOR EATING HIS MEATLOAF?
EXACTLY!
DON'T WORRY, WEENIE. WE'LL BE WITH YOU EVERY STEP OF THE WAY, WON'T WE, FRANK?
I SUPPOSE.
HURRAH FOR THE OTHER THING THAT IS BETTER THAN MEATLOAF . . .

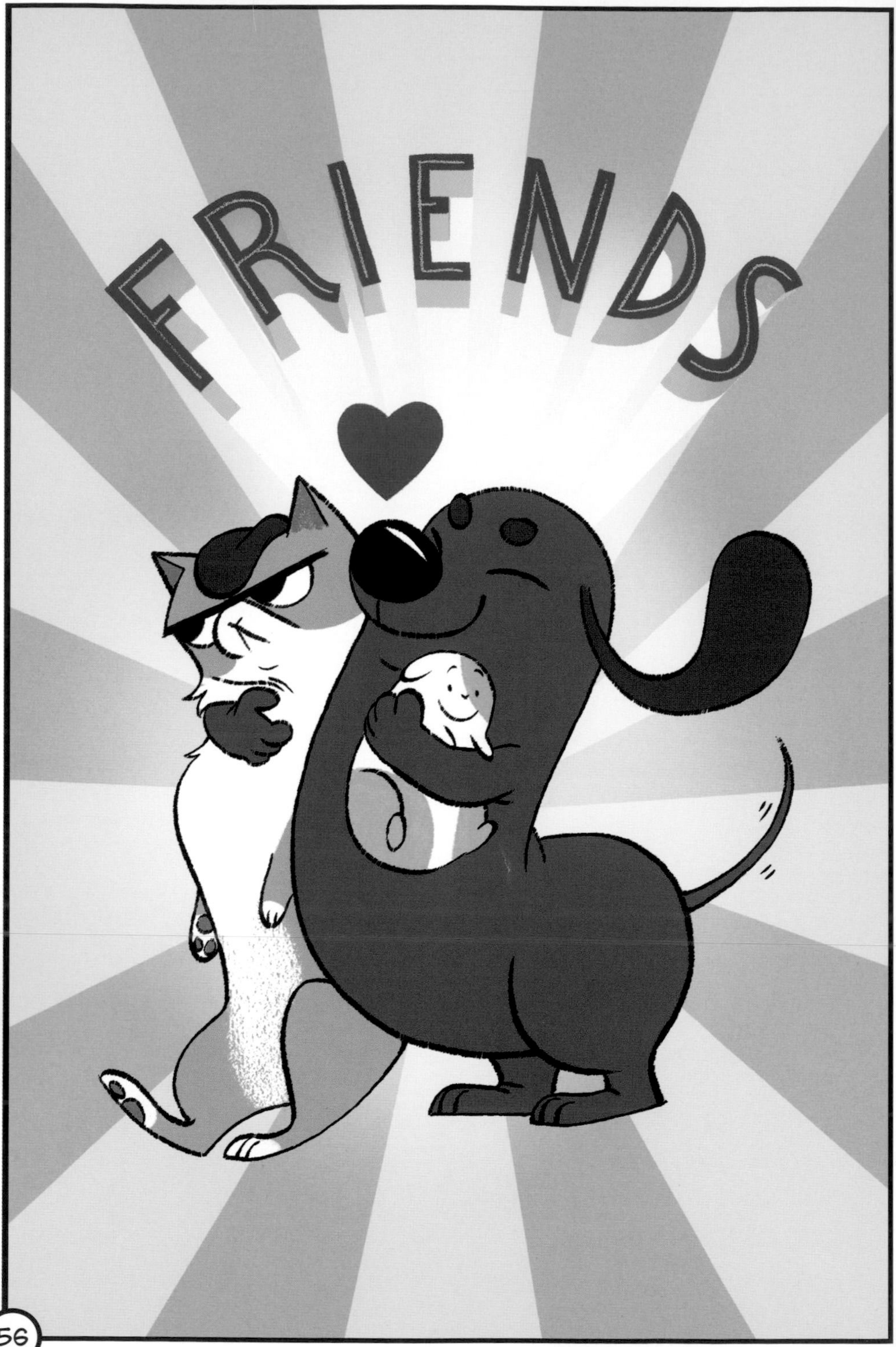
FRIENDS